WEDDINGS ARE MURDER

When DI Casey Clunes visits Oakham Manor with a view to holding her wedding there, the last thing she expects to discover is a body. Planning her big day quickly takes second place to solving a murder ... A woman disappears from her family home in mysterious circumstances — but are the grieving family victims, or villains? And what is so important about the contents of some old love letters, that their now-famous author will go to any lengths to stop them being made public?

GERALDINE RYAN

◆

WEDDINGS ARE MURDER
AND OTHER STORIES

Complete and Unabridged

LINFORD
Leicester

First published in Great Britain

First Linford Edition
published 2016

A catalogue record for this book is available
from the British Library.

ISBN 978–1–4448–2809–2

Published by
F. A. Thorpe (Publishing)
Anstey, Leicestershire

Set by Words & Graphics Ltd.
Anstey, Leicestershire
Printed and bound in Great Britain by
T. J. International Ltd., Padstow, Cornwall

This book is printed on acid-free paper

Contents

Weddings are Murder

PowerPoint presentations! How Casey loathed them. Surely there must be a more exciting way of disseminating information about alcohol duty fraud, she mused as she doodled a third row of wineglasses in her notebook. A quick glance round the table told her what she already suspected — everyone else was bored stiff too. The Super actually had his eyes closed!

'Any questions at this stage?' The appropriately named Jody Bright, who was the young detective constable giving the presentation, glanced hopefully round the room.

Tentatively, Casey raised her hand. This was going to be awkward.

'DI Clunes?'

'Er — I'm really sorry, Jody. Only I've got to be somewhere in about ten minutes and . . . '

A low rumble of laughter travelled

round the room.

'Oh, sorry. Yes. Of course,' said Jody, looking somewhat crestfallen.

'But it's all been very useful, I'm sure we all agree,' Casey said diplomatically, as she hastily collected her things and made her way out.

The silence behind her was deafening.

★　★　★

Casey's appointment with Alicia Nunn wasn't for another half hour, and Devden was less than fifteen minutes away, so she needn't have left the meeting when she did. But Alicia wasn't the only person she'd arranged to see. Dom would be there too — at least he'd better be.

Get to the venue at 3.15, she'd reminded him last night, knowing that punctuality wasn't exactly her fiancé's forte. According to Alicia, they should come to this meeting with a few ideas of their own. After all, it was *their* wedding. It wasn't her way to steamroll over couples' ideas with her own, she'd told Casey over the phone.

Casey had tried to get Dom to sit down and discuss what they both wanted so many times since she'd made that first initial enquiry about the possibility of holding their nuptials at Oakham Manor. But time after time something cropped up, and they never got further than agreeing that they wanted a party with a cake, speeches, and lots of booze.

The thing about Dom — and this was what made him unusual among men — was that he was totally unsusceptible to female wiles. To this day he insisted that the reason he'd fallen for Casey was her openness and complete lack of guile.

But the thing about Alicia was that she came across as very wily indeed. Even from their brief phone conversation, Casey was fully aware of what they'd be up against when they actually met face to face — the hard sell dressed up as a charm offensive. But if Dom suspected this as well, Casey knew he'd say he wasn't interested. If she could just persuade him to stay long enough to listen to Alicia's spiel, then he might come round to her way of thinking.

Which was that since neither of them had the first idea about how to organise a kid's birthday party, let alone a wedding, then the most sensible solution — albeit the most expensive one — would be to leave it to the professionals.

With every passing glimpse of the land encircling Oakham Manor this snaking drive inland afforded her, the more anxious she became. Here was a flash of undulating green — the stunning golf course laid out to professional standard; round the next bend a flight of swans swooping down from the sky went skittering along the shivering lake, grey in the winter afternoon. Visible from every turn of the road was the crenellated tower of Oakham Manor Folly — a black finger pointing up toward the lowering sky. Then finally the manor house, peeping through the grove of evergreens that until this moment had hidden it from Casey's view. As she wound her way up the sweeping drive, its full majestic beauty hit her like a sock in the jaw.

What on earth had she been thinking of? Having the wedding here would fleece them. Though she hadn't yet discussed money with Alicia, she'd optimistically talked herself into believing it would be affordable. Loads of quite ordinary people got married here all the time, after all. But as she followed the signs to the car park she remembered that chat she'd had with Gail Carter over lunch in the canteen last week, and the doubts began to flood in.

'You do know what you're letting yourselves in for, don't you?' she'd said in the manner of a person who'd been there, done that and was still paying off the bills. 'You won't see much change out of twelve grand if you're thinking of getting married at Oakham Manor. Maybe nearer fifteen even.'

Till that moment Casey had assumed that getting married was simply a matter of buying a ring and a new frock and saying *I do* in front of a few friends. Dom, even more naively, still basked under the illusion that the biggest expense was the license fee. She'd almost choked on a lettuce leaf.

'Just think about it. The drinks bill

alone will bankrupt you once that lot get near the bar,' Gail said, jerking her head in the direction of the table behind, where several of their male colleagues were enjoying the unhealthy option, as usual.

'Well, Oakham Manor is just an idea,' Casey said. 'All we're doing is having a look round.'

'Fair enough. But the trouble is, once you see it you'll be sold, and everything afterwards will be a let-down.'

As Casey climbed out of the car she reminded herself again that she was only looking. Predictably, there was no sign of Dom. She wondered about texting him; but then if he were already on his way, he wouldn't read it. What if she were to have a little look round inside herself first? The winter sun held little warmth at this time of day and she suspected it would be much cosier inside.

The plush reception area was quiet apart from the tinkly piano musack emanating from the speakers. Weddings were a seasonal affair, and February meant little activity on that front. She was aware that Oakham Manor was also a popular venue for corporate events, but nothing of that ilk was going on here today.

'Can I help you?'

The speaker was an elegantly turned-out young woman sitting behind the desk, who'd broken off from typing something into her laptop at Casey's entrance. The name badge on the lapel of her dove-grey jacket said Kathy Ling.

Casey introduced herself, substituting Ms Clunes for DI Clunes. Disclosing her profession invariably put the wind up people, she always found.

'I have an appointment with Alicia Nunn,' she said, 'although I'm a bit previous.'

Kathy smiled brightly. 'Right,' she said. 'I'll just ring through.'

While she waited, Casey wondered about ringing Dom again. She'd give him five minutes, she decided. By which time he would officially be late.

'I'm afraid she's not picking up her phone,' Kathy said. 'I'm ever so sorry. I could try another number in case she's with the manager . . . '

The main door swung open with a clatter, cutting off whatever it was that Kathy had been about to say. A rather dishevelled-looking woman of indeterminate age dressed in overalls, with her hair scraped back off her face, stood there struggling to get her breath.

'Nina! You know not to use this entrance.' Kathy's tone was muted and polite but her expression betrayed her fury at this transgression.

'Kathy. Lady.' The woman's heavily accented voice shook as she glanced from Kathy to Casey and then back again. 'You must come. It's Alicia. Something terrible has happened to her.'

★   ★   ★

'Bit of a stroke of luck, you being on the scene like that,' the Super said, glancing up from his newspaper.

From where Casey was standing on the other side of his desk, the headlines on the front page of the *Brockhaven Gazette* were clearly visible. *Wedding planner, 32, found dead at foot of folly*, she read. It was quite a tongue-twister.

'Strictly speaking, Alicia Nunn's full title was 'events organiser', Casey said glumly. 'But factual accuracy was never the *Gazette*'s main concern.'

'Didn't your man Dom used to write for them, till he became a fully-fledged author and a radio presenter?'

Dom had had some success with a book — a comic account of his days as a journalist, entitled *Headlines and By-lines* — which in turn had led to a regular gig on local radio. The money wasn't fantastic, but what they'd lost on his regular income they gained in free childcare. These days Casey was the main breadwinner and Dom had assumed the role of house husband.

'He used to be their crime reporter. I was a detective constable back then. That's how we met. He was always pestering me for stories. And dates.'

'The rest, as they say, is history. How's the little fella?'

The 'little fella' was Finlay — four years old, and the apple of Casey's eye. Dom's too, of course. It was mostly because of Finlay that she and Dom had decided that perhaps they really ought to start thinking seriously about tying the knot. Finlay would be off to school soon, and though neither of them was overly concerned with convention, they both agreed that being married might just make life simpler all round.

'Finlay's great,' Casey said. 'Especially after a day dealing with some of the cases we have. Going home to him makes you feel clean again.'

The Super nodded sympathetically. 'So. This girl. It's an unusual death, right? Any news on the post-mortem?'

'I wish.' Casey raised her eyes heavenwards. 'It's been five days now and we're still waiting to hear, both from the pathologist and the forensics department.'

The last thing she wanted was to get into another conversation about the Super's hobby-horse — the dreaded cutbacks. The best thing was to deflect him, she decided. Tell him what they *had* managed to do, not what they'd so far failed to.

'She's been identified by her parents.

Understandably, they're still in shock. I think PC Carter accompanied them.'

'Gail? Good. Local people, are they?'

'They live in Brockhaven. As does her sister, apparently. The parents had very little to do with her, according to Gail. She got the impression there'd been a falling-out some time before. But when she asked if they knew of any reason their daughter might take her own life, they were horrified. I believe they're both big in their local church community. Suicide doesn't play well in those circles.'

'Quite. And the sister? Older? Younger? Close?'

'Not sure. Too shocked to say anything much, according to Gail. Though she did hint that Alicia had left her last job because she wanted to get away from a man. A *married* man. Which may well have been the reason for the family squabble. She'd only been working at Oakham Manor for six months or so. It was a new start for her, apparently.'

'A married man, eh?' The Super steepled his hands and gazed into the distance. 'You think she may have decided her life wasn't worth living without this man in it?'

'I don't think anything, sir,' Casey said. 'I'd rather wait to hear what the pathologist comes up with.'

Casey had always considered herself hardened by death. But running pell-mell towards the folly tower with Kathy Ling and Nina Marek hot on her heels, she hadn't known what to expect. The broken body of Alicia Nunn, her limbs splayed at odd angles, her eyes wide open and staring up at the sky, had shocked even her hardened soul. Since then the memory of her lying there had seared itself onto the inside of her eyelids and become the last thing she saw just before falling asleep.

The Super's phone started ringing, cutting into Casey's thoughts. She gave herself a mental shake as he reached out and took hold of the receiver. 'I'll be on my way,' she mouthed, but he held up a hand to stop her. She remained where she was, studying his face, which was a picture of intense concentration. When he put down the phone he smiled at her so broadly his eyes crinkled in the corners.

'Good news, sir?'

'I don't know about that, Casey, but I think we can safely say that our Miss Nunn didn't die of natural causes.'

Casey's heartbeat quickened.

'She was wearing a jacket when she fell. And according to forensics, there's a handprint on it.'

It took a moment for this to compute. 'You mean she was pushed?'

The Super nodded. 'Looks like we've got a murder investigation on our hands.'

'In that case I'll set up the incident room right away,' said Casey.

★   ★   ★

What had Alicia been doing at the top of the folly tower anyway, on a cold winter's day, when she could have been sitting in a nice warm office? Was it a place of refuge? Or had she arranged to meet someone there? And speaking of busy schedules, how many appointments had she had on the day she died, apart from the one with Casey and Dom, and with whom?

15

Forensics had failed to come up with any diary, so either she kept this information stored on her computer — which they were still examining — or the diary had disappeared.

Casey needed to go back to the hotel and interview the people Alicia had worked with before people's memories dimmed. She would have liked to take Gail with her, but since news of their daughter's murder had come through, Gail had officially been assigned to Mr and Mrs Nunn as police liaison officer.

Casey's head told her that Jody Bright was the girl for the job. But her heart sank at the prospect. An afternoon in Jody's company could be exhausting. She never took a moment off.

In a bid to delay the inevitable, she decided to play the video of the CCTV footage they'd just got hold of. Cameras were thin on the ground at Oakham Manor, but fortunately there did happen to be one in position at the front of the building that looked out onto the drive. With a bit of luck the killer might be caught approaching — something that would make everybody's jobs easier.

Casey pressed play and waited for something to happen. Watch any TV cop drama and CCTV came over as clear as daylight. The cops had the culprit banged to rights before you could say high definition. But in real life what you got at best was shadowy movement, flickers, blurs. And that was on a good day. She'd lost count of how many times in the old days, before they'd learned to speed the tape up effectively, she'd sat through two hours of blank screen.

There was a sharp rap on her office door. Without waiting for a summons, Jody put her head round it. Casey summoned up a generous welcome. 'Come and have a look at this footage,' she said.

Jody was already pulling up a chair. Casey mentally chastised herself for being so mealy-mouthed at this young CD's enthusiasm. She was getting jaded, she decided.

She pressed play and zoomed through. According to forensics, the time of death was between 11 a.m. and 2.30 p.m. She'd been found just minutes after Casey had introduced herself at reception. She knew for a fact the time then had been 3.10.

'Nothing, nothing, nothing,' she muttered as she zoomed through shots of the front of the house. A delivery van drew up but disappeared around the back at 8.10.

'Why didn't they have a camera positioned at the back entrance?' Jody asked, echoing Casey's thoughts.

'We'll get nothing from this,' Casey said glumly. Then, 'Hang on, what's this? A car.' She brightened up considerably. 'Recognise the make? Looks like a Toyota Corolla.' She peered at the screen. 2 p.m. She stopped the tape.

'What's he doing? Is he getting out?' Jody asked.

'I don't know.'

'Well move it on, then.'

Casey's finger hovered over play. Before she could press the key, an impatient Jody jumped in and pressed it for her. Yes, it was a Toyota Corolla all right. Together they studied the screen, waiting for something to happen.

'He's not getting out,' Jody said as,

after fifteen minutes on the timer had passed, the driver drove away.

'Tell you what,' Casey said, switching off the computer, 'let's leave this boring stuff to uniform. Why don't you drive over to Oakham Manor with me and help me conduct some interviews?'

'Cool,' Jody said.

Well, thought Casey, jumping up and grabbing her coat, *I'm glad one of us is.*

★ ★ ★

'So what else do we know so far from forensics?' Jody, at the wheel of the car they'd been assigned, liked asking questions. Fortunately, Casey was still smart enough to answer most of them.

'That the fingerprints on Alicia Nunn's jacket weren't hers and didn't belong to Nina Marek either. That her phone's gone missing, which could be important. And that she has fibres under her nails that are suggestive of a struggle.'

'Suspects?'

'Everyone who worked there or who visited Oakham Manor on the day of her

19

murder,' Casey said. 'Including me, I suppose.'

Jody looked askance at her. 'Aw, come on,' she said. 'Your bloke too?'

The less said about that the better, Casey decided. Dom was still insisting that he'd forgotten all about it. Until the moment she'd watched that CCTV footage and seen his car parked in front of Oakham Manor as clear as the nose on her face, she'd believed him. But what now?

'Pull up over there, would you? Just in front of the main reception area.'

'Right, boss.'

'First stop, the manager: Robert Castle. Been in charge here years. Let's go.'

But before either of them were out of the car, Casey's phone burst into life. It was Dom. She had to take this.

'Look, Jody,' she said, 'how about having a nose around on your own? Make your way over to the tower and familiarise yourself with the landscape. I'll come and find you when I'm done.'

'Right you are, boss.' Jody strode off with her usual enthusiasm, leaving Casey staring at her phone, totally unprepared for how to handle this phone call.

'Dom,' she said coolly, 'what's up?'

The silence on the end seemed to last forever. 'We need to talk,' he said at last.

'I think we do,' she agreed. 'I've just seen CCTV of your car standing in the driveway of Oakham Manor on the day a murder was committed.'

'Yes. The thought occurred to me that you might have. That's why I'm calling you.'

'You told me you'd forgotten all about our meeting.'

'I know. It looks bad, doesn't it? Technically, I must be a suspect.'

'Yes.'

She wasn't going to say anything else. Let Dom talk. Let him explain himself. He had a great deal of it to do, lying to her like that. There was another long silence. She waited. And waited. Finally Dom began to explain.

'I came early. Finlay was at nursery, and I thought if I drove out there and had a look at the place I'd be able to see if I could imagine us getting married there, before the wedding planner started giving us her spiel. I mean, I'm sorry she's dead and all, but I've met a few events organisers in my time and frankly they all set my teeth on edge.'

Well, she'd been right about his reaction to Alicia Nunn, then.

'I couldn't see it, Casey.'

'What do you mean?'

'This wedding. I sat in the car and thought, no. This isn't me. It isn't us.'

Casey thought her heart was about to stop. 'You don't want to get married?'

'Yes. Yes I do.'

Relief flooded into her.

'But I don't want someone else planning it for us.'

'But we're rubbish at that stuff. Remember the mess we made of Finlay's last birthday party?' Half the mothers at playgroup were still crossing the road to avoid them.

'But that's us, Casey. We're not perfect. Our house is a mess. But we're happy like that. Let's do it ourselves. Take a risk. See where it leads.'

Casey was relenting. Dom always had

that effect on her.

'We'll see. We'll talk about it tonight, shall we? I've got to go now. My DC's trying to get my attention.'

Jody looked perkier than ever as she strode back towards Casey. 'Boss,' she called out, 'I've found something interesting. You've got to take a look at this!'

'A bicycle key!' Casey slipped her phone back into her pocket, reminding herself she was here to investigate a murder, not to discuss options for a wedding ceremony. It was high time she shelved her private life and concentrated on the job that was — literally — in hand. Jody's outstretched, gloved hand to be precise. 'Where did you find it?' she wanted to know.

Jody launched into a detailed and lengthy explanation. She'd walked round the tower a few times, though she'd been prevented from actually climbing it because of the police tape at the entrance. Speculating that if the murderer had come from a direction other than that of Oakham Manor, and hadn't gone back there once they'd despatched poor Alicia

23

Nunn — and it would be a cool customer who would be able to do that, she added — then where had they come from, and how had they got away unnoticed?

'They could have gone two ways,' she said, answering her own question. 'Back towards Brockhaven and the coast, or inland through Devden and then on to . . . well, anywhere, I guess. You'd need a car to get away from the area altogether, but Brockhaven and the next couple of villages inland are reachable on foot by anybody with a reasonable level of fitness.'

'Even easier to reach by bike,' Casey mumbled.

'To get back to Brockhaven you could cut across the golf course or go through the wood, or you could go round by the lake towards the main road,' Jody said. Totally ignoring Casey's previous remark, she pointed this way and that. 'I just went as far as that little gate behind the tower that takes you onto the track, and looked round. Which is what I assumed forensics would have done. And there it was.'

'Of course, there's nothing to say this

is evidence,' Casey said. 'If forensics didn't see it, then maybe it wasn't there when they looked. It could be a perfectly innocent key dropped by a perfectly innocent cyclist on any day and at any time since the murder took place.'

'So, what now?' Jody asked, suddenly dejected.

'Interviews, I think,' said Casey. 'Follow me.'

* * *

Casey's first impression of the man who'd been Alicia Nunn's line manager was of a person out of his depth. Sitting at his desk in his large, airy office looking out over the golf green, Robert Castle constantly fidgeted with anything and everything in reach. He seemed incapable of answering any of the questions put to him in a straightforward manner. Even the simplest ones led back to this: everyone at Oakham Manor loved Alicia. It was inconceivable that her life had been cut short in such a brutal manner. On the day of her murder there had only been a skeleton staff present, he said. What with the time of year and the recession, business wasn't that great. That was why his superiors had brought in new staff, Castle said — a touch resentfully, Casey thought; Alicia to put the oomph back into managing events and Silas Burns, the new chef, to do the same for the catering, which had fallen off in recent years. Besides those two and himself, there wouldn't have been more than an additional half-dozen or so others around on that day — the groundsmen, a few kitchen staff, the cleaners . . . oh, and Kathy Ling, whom he believed DCI Clunes had already met.

'Where were you on the day Miss Nunn died?' Jody cut to the chase. 'In your office all day?'

Castle, clearly prepared for this, pushed his diary across the desk, the relevant page bound open with an elastic band. It was one of those hour-by-hour ones, and every hour seemed to have been accounted for. Although there was nothing to say he couldn't have filled in these times in arrears, of course.

'I have nothing to hide, Officer,' he said. 'I can talk you through each one of these meetings and give you the contact number of everyone I spoke to on that day too. Nina might have brought me a coffee or two,' he added. 'Obviously I wouldn't have pencilled *that* in. I'm often accused of being a stickler for detail, but even I would draw the line there.' He sat back and chuckled at his own joke. 'Apart from that, it's all here.' He pointed to the evening slot — 8 p.m. 'Look here — I've pencilled in my date with Alicia too. It would have been our second,' he added mournfully.

'Really?' *This could be interesting*, Casey thought.

'We'll take this, please.' Jody picked up the diary and slipped it into her bag. Casey wondered if Robert Castle was having the same effect on Jody that he was having on herself. There was something slightly unctuous about him. He was a man bending over backwards to be helpful.

'We'll get back to you later if we have any other questions,' Casey said. She put

27

out her hand and looked him squarely in the face. 'Which I'm sure we will,' she added. 'Meanwhile, if you'll excuse us . . . ' It was a relief when he released Casey's hand from his damp grip and the door to his office finally stood between them.

'I don't trust him an inch,' Jody whispered once they were outside. 'Shifty. Plus, I've seen a picture of Alicia Nunn, and she's way out of his league.'

'While that may be correct,' Casey said, 'it doesn't make him a murderer.' Jody gave a sigh of disappointment. It must be such hard work being her, Casey mused. 'Patience is a virtue, Jody. We'll get there, even if it's slowly,' she promised.

A look of pure dejection flitted across Jody's face before her default setting of looking on the bright side took hold once more. 'I wonder if the boys back at the station have come up with any information on that Toyota Corolla yet,' she said. 'It might be worth giving them a ring.'

Casey's heart sank. 'Er, about that, Jody . . . ' she said.

Where to start?

It was a relief to shut the door behind those two police officers. Robert Castle opened the drawer to his desk, took out a half-full bottle of vodka and a glass, and poured himself a generous measure. He needed it to steady his nerves, he told himself. It wasn't as if he were an alcoholic or anything.

It wasn't a lie, what he'd told those two. Not really. He *would* have seen Alicia that evening had things not turned out as they had. And he *had* gone for a drink with her the previous week out at the Old Oak in Devden village. But to maintain that that had been a date . . . well, maybe that could have been a slight exaggeration.

'I wonder if I could speak to you about something,' she'd said, popping her head round his office door that day, just as he was about to ring Silas and have a word with him about his ridiculous choice of menu for the Rotarians' AGM. More fancy New World dishes, most of which he'd either never heard of or was unable to pronounce.

She wanted to ask him a favour, she'd said. Was he free later? That was when he'd come up with the idea of a drink. He'd been more than a bit taken aback by the ready way she agreed. He wasn't used to girls being so keen to go out with him. She must really like him, he decided.

He'd thought so again later, in the pub. All the signs were there — the way she'd laughed at his jokes, leaning in close and hanging on to his to every word. What a fool he'd been. She made that pretty clear next day. Then Silas Burns had to come and stick his egomaniacal nose in where it wasn't wanted.

Robert poured himself another drink. Thinking of Silas always got him worked up. That little favour Alicia had wanted to ask him . . . He must have agreed to it, but he was damned if he could remember what it was till the following day when she'd reminded him of it. That was when it had all gone wrong — and he'd had to explain that actually, what she'd asked him was way out of his remit. He didn't have that sort of authority.

How angry she'd got then. Shaking

with fury. But he'd *said*. He'd *promised*. She'd said some other stuff too. Terrible, wounding things. About rumours she'd heard and had tried to ignore but now knew were true. Blaming him for Oakham Manor going down the pan, as she described it. Calling him incompetent. Worse — a *lush*. Of course he'd reacted. What man wouldn't? He'd been driven over the edge.

And then Silas had shown up. The maniac. God knew what would have happened if Kathy hadn't intervened.

Later, when it was all over and things had calmed down, he'd gone back into his room and helped himself to a couple of stiffeners. Perhaps if he'd had a coffee instead, he wouldn't have taken out his diary and pencilled in those words for that day almost a week ago now — the day that she'd died. *Drinks with Alicia.* Wishful thinking.

★   ★   ★

Jody had gone quiet since Casey's revelation that the Toyota Corolla in the

31

CCTV video had belonged to none other than the man Casey shared her life with. That was the difference between DC Bright and PC Gail Carter. Gail would have found the whole thing hilarious. Jody, on the other hand, had probably already decided on Dom's motive and was wondering when they could pick him up and slap the cuffs on him.

'We need to talk to Kathy Ling — find out Alicia's schedule on the day she died,' Casey said in a bid to distract her. 'I know I'm the first to moan when the Super starts banging on about cutbacks; but really, he has a point. Outsourcing our tech services to some computer geeks over in Cambridge is a flaming joke.'

Jody shot her a look of concern. 'Are you okay, Casey?' she said. 'I know you've got a lot of personal stuff on your mind.'

Oh my God, thought Casey. The girl actually *did* believe that stuff about Dom. Worse, she probably thought that Casey believed it too, and was finding it impossible to concentrate on anything else while suspicion hung over him.

'I'm fine,' Casey said. 'I'm just not

prepared to wait any longer for them to get off their backsides and help us out. Sometimes it's quicker to do things the traditional way.'

'Right.'

'Look, Jody,' she added, 'if it makes you feel any better, do feel free to haul Dom in for questioning.'

'Don't be silly. I was only joking.' Jody was clearly embarrassed.

Honestly, the girl was the giddy limit . . . But maybe not. Maybe she was just doing her job and should be praised for treating everybody the same, no matter what their status or who they happened to share a bed with. 'No, really,' Casey said. 'We need to follow procedure if we want to avoid accusations of police corruption. And I'm sure he'll be more than happy to give you a DNA sample so he can rule himself out.'

'I thought you'd see it like that, boss,' Jody said, pleased with herself for showing some initiative. 'Now, is it this way to reception?'

★　★　★

33

'So, I was Alicia's only appointment that afternoon — nobody else?'

'I'll just check.' Click, click, click. Kathy's eyes travelled back and forth across the computer screen. 'Sometimes Alicia didn't always bother to let me know who was coming,' she said finally, looking up.

'Great!' Jody didn't bother to hide her irritation. 'So she could have had twenty visitors that day and you wouldn't have known anything about it.'

'I would have seen them,' said Kathy, polite as ever, 'if I was here at my desk.'

'And how often are you not at your desk?' Jody wanted to know.

There was a long pause. 'I may not have been here all the time on the morning that Alicia died,' Kathy said at last.

'Because?' Jody said.

Kathy was hiding something, Casey was convinced. She decided to change the subject briefly. 'You must be suffering with the recession,' she said chattily.

Jody looked askance at her. Casey returned a look of her own. It said, *trust me, I know what I'm doing.*

'A bit. Plus it's low season too,' Kathy said. 'But next week we've got the Rotarian AGM and a couple of conferences. Our first spring wedding isn't for a few weeks, but after that I'm sure it'll be all go.'

Casey doubted that. She couldn't vouch for other prospective brides, but frankly, she'd gone right off the idea of getting married in a place where someone had been murdered. As omens went, it was a pretty potent one. 'Tell me the drill, Kathy,' she said. 'I need to get a feel for Alicia's job and her day-to-day routine. If, for example, my appointment with her had actually gone ahead and I'd decided I liked the look of this place, how would we have proceeded?'

'Alicia was very hands-on,' Kathy said. 'There would have been lots of meetings and plenty of emails flying around. She starts — started — months in advance, and you would have made several visits yourself to discuss the details.'

'I see.'

'Then there were the pre-wedding

tastings. That was something Alicia introduced. She encouraged the bride and groom to invite their parents along to sample the dishes so they could settle on the best choice.'

'Must have led to a few ding-dongs,' Casey said with a smile.

'I guess.' Kathy was totally relaxed now. 'But sometimes parents are a bit more interested in fine food and wines than the kids.' She seemed to remember something. 'The first couple getting married in the spring, for instance. I think the bride's father is some sort of wine buff. Worked for Draper's, so he must have known what he was talking about.' Draper's was a long-established brewery and wine-importing business based in Brockhaven. Most of the pubs in the region were Draper's pubs.

'Was she happy here?' Casey asked, bringing the subject back to Alicia.

Kathy considered the question. 'I'd say so,' she said. 'She used to get stressed at times keeping on top of the details. But when the day itself had come and gone and the thank-you emails arrived and the good reviews appeared on the website, she used to say it was worth all the hassle.'

'Why did you leave your desk that day, Kathy? Was it for a long time?' Casey's question came from so out of the blue that Kathy's inscrutable professional façade was momentarily cracked.

'There was a disturbance,' she said, keeping her eyes lowered. 'One of the kitchen staff — Nina — came to get me. She said Silas — the chef — had a kitchen knife and was waving it about.' She didn't really know what the argument was about even now, she continued, not having been there at the start. Nina might be in a better position to throw light on it; but when Kathy had arrived at the scene, Robert, Alicia and Silas were all outside the kitchen and there was a lot of shouting going on. To be fair, she said, the fact that Silas had a knife in his hand could simply have meant that he'd been in the middle of chopping something up and had just been drawn out of the kitchen by the sound of raised voices. 'But I was scared,' Kathy said. 'I didn't

37

know what he might do next.'

'Not surprising,' Casey said.

'Oh, I wish Nina were here. She'd back me up. She did tell me what she'd overheard though.'

'Which was?' Casey asked.

'She said she heard Alicia calling Robert a lush. She asked me what it meant because she'd never heard the word before. I didn't tell her because I didn't know myself till later when I looked it up. Robert started shouting back at Alicia, which was when Nina came running down the corridor to see what was going on. When she got there, there was Silas, with the knife. That's when she came running for me.'

'You don't look big enough to take on two big strapping men,' Jody said, grinning broadly.

'Actually I'm a karate black belt,' Kathy said politely but unsmilingly.

Things were getting even more complicated! Could *she* have pushed Alicia over the side of the tower? Casey wondered. Her loyalty to her boss seemed unwavering, it occurred to her. Maybe she was jealous of whatever was going on between him and Alicia. 'Robert told us that he'd recently started seeing Alicia. Were you aware of that, Miss Ling?' Kathy widened her eyes. 'You seem surprised.'

'I am. In fact, I couldn't be more surprised.' Her calm, professional exterior was visibly crumbling. Kathy knew a heck of a lot more than she was letting on, Casey was convinced.

'I should tell you . . . ' Kathy said at last. *A-ha! Now we're getting somewhere*, thought Casey. ' . . . Robert *did* like Alicia. It was an open secret. Everywhere she went he followed her like a puppy. She told me she didn't like it. Went out of her way to avoid him, in fact. But then something happened. She changed towards him. Started flirting. It was weird. Particularly since . . . well, she and Silas were seeing each other.'

'Really?' Jody wasn't exactly rubbing her hands together in glee, but she might as well have been.

Kathy looked suddenly frightened. 'If Silas had got wind of the change in Alicia, who knows what he might have been capable of. I've seen him in a fury. I wouldn't want to be on the other end of it.'

* * *

'Brandishing a knife? What utter nonsense!'

Standing there in the middle of his kitchen, dressed in his chef whites, Silas Burns, all six foot plus of him, cut an attractive, self-assured figure. Was he denying he'd been carrying a knife when he came bursting out of the kitchen? Jody demanded. He flinched at her question.

'Look,' he said, 'I don't know what people have been saying about me. Okay, I've got a temper. But I'm a chef. I use knives. I heard a row. I was curious. I came out to see what was going on, still holding the knife I'd been chopping vegetables with.'

'And what *was* going on?' Casey asked.

'I suspect Alicia was giving Robert Castle a few home truths,' he replied. 'He'd promised to do something and he'd failed to deliver, was what I gathered. Par

40

for the course. The man is a complete loser. The management only put up with him because he's family.'

That explained it. 'I'm a bit confused,' Casey said. 'I'm hearing two different things. One, that she was going out with you. The other, that Castle was her boyfriend.'

'In his dreams,' he said.

'So she was your girlfriend, then?' Jody said.

'Mine?' He seemed taken aback. 'Look, Alicia was a lovely young woman. We spent a lot of time together. But only ever as friends. Besides,' he added, 'I think Alicia was already taken.' Casey and Jody exchanged a glance. 'I don't know if I should be saying this,' he mumbled. 'But my room looks out over the back. The unglamorous bit of Oakham Manor, you might say. It's where the smokers go for their breaks.'

And Alicia was a smoker. Casey knew that from the post-mortem.

'I saw her out there one night. She seemed agitated. Kept checking her phone a lot. Then this car drew up. Jazzy affair.

41

She went running towards it and got in. Great big grin on her face. He stuck his face out the window and she kissed him.'

'So you got a glimpse of him?' asked Casey.

'Not much of one. She was all over him straight away. But I do wonder if I might have seen the guy before. He may have been a guest. We get a lot passing through, as I'm sure you can imagine.'

'Can you describe him?' Jody asked.

'A lot older than her. Suit. Tie. Have you ever heard a man described as a silver fox? Well, that was him. Nigel Havers type. You can see why young women would be attracted.'

'Thank you, Mr Burns,' Casey said. 'Thank you very much.'

Maybe it was high time she found out a bit more about Alicia Nunn's complicated love life, Casey thought as she and Jody made their way outside.

* * *

Casey was sitting at the dining room table amid the debris of her dinner, trying to make some sort of sense from all the disparate pieces of information she'd received so far about Alicia Nunn. Every now and again Dom came through from the kitchen, collecting dirty dishes at a leisurely pace.

Alicia was well-liked, according to Robert Castle. By all accounts he liked her a bit *too* well, but the feeling wasn't reciprocated. Until she wanted a favour. When the favour wasn't delivered she appeared to have given up pretending she even liked the man. But if she'd been universally liked, she wouldn't have been found dead at the bottom of the folly tower, so what Castle said wasn't the whole truth.

Casey had written Alicia's name in the middle of a blank page and ringed it. She was the spider in her diagram. To Robert Castle, who was one of the legs, she added the name Silas Burns, another leg. One night, looking out of his window, he'd seen Alicia snogging the face off an older man. A *silver fox* was how he'd described him. Was this the married man Gail had heard about from Alicia's sister?

43

Who was he, this married man? How could she find out? If Alicia had confided to her sister that she was having an affair, she may well have revealed the man's name. With the sister and the married man you got two more spider's legs.

And that brought her to yet another couple: the parents. God-fearing folk who disapproved of their daughter's behaviour. But disapproved strongly enough to kill her? Gail would have a feeling about it, she was sure. As soon as she could tomorrow, Casey would corner her and pick her brains.

And what did Kathy Ling — the karate black belt — have against Alicia? she asked herself as she sketched another leg and abutted it with the initials KL. Would she have admitted that if she was guilty of Alicia's murder? It would be the first thing to draw suspicion. Unless, of course, it was a double bluff.

She sighed loudly. If only they had some hard evidence. Where was Alicia's phone? Why was CCTV so lax? Why had nobody seen anything?

'I've been thinking.' Dom had made his final trip to the kitchen and returned with a bottle of red wine and two glasses, which he set down on the table.

'Me too,' she muttered. 'And it's not helped.'

'Not about murder,' Dom said, opening the bottle with steady concentration. 'But about marriage.'

Casey glanced up at him curiously. She never understood why he still insisted on buying the ones with corks instead of screw tops. She put it down to his superior education.

'We could get married at my old college,' he said. 'St Mike's.'

'Cambridge University?' Casey was slack-jawed at the suggestion. 'Can you do that?'

Dom poured the wine at long last. 'Well, I'm a graduate. And St Mike's has got a chapel and a Great Hall.'

'What's great about it?' Casey wanted to know.

Dom sighed dramatically. 'It's *called* the Great Hall. It's the dining room. Stained-glass windows. Art all over the

45

walls, oak tables, the lot.'

'Pardon my ignorance.' Casey took a sip of her wine.

'There would be staff to wait at tables. Fabulous wines — the wine cellar at St Mike's is famous. All we'd need to do is decide on the date, the menu and the guest list.'

'Flowers,' Casey said. 'We'd have to do flowers. And seating arrangements. And organise the disco afterwards. Do they do discos at Cambridge colleges?'

'There's a huge events room at the student union anyone can hire as long as it's not term time; and since the undergraduates are only up for twenty-four weeks a year, that should be easy enough to manage.'

Up? Did people still say *up?* Apparently so.

'So what do you think?' he asked.

Casey pondered Dom's suggestion. She'd been to St Mike's once on a nostalgic visit. Nostalgic for Dom, not for her. She'd tried to hate it, not being a fan of privilege for the few and glass ceilings for the masses. But much to her own chagrin, she'd fallen in love with it immediately.

'I think it sounds like a plan,' she said.

Dom was obviously thrilled she'd agreed so readily. He'd been expecting a fight, he said. 'So, now that's settled, all you have to do is work out who murdered Alicia Nunn.'

'Simples,' said Casey in her meerkat voice.

★ ★ ★

Next morning, Casey and Jody returned to Oakham Manor to finish interviewing the staff who'd been off duty the previous day. It was a morning that was fast turning into a day as long and fruitless as the previous one. It seemed that no one had seen or heard anything out of the ordinary that morning.

It was the argument between Silas, Robert and Alicia that was responsible for that, Casey was convinced. An armed robbery could have taken place and people wouldn't have noticed. Everybody was far too caught up with gossiping about the row to bother taking much notice of the unauthorised comings and goings of various visitors.

Kathy Ling, by her own admission, had been so shaken up at the sight of Silas Burns brandishing the kitchen knife that she'd taken herself off to a quiet corner of the morning room with a pot of strong coffee. One of the kitchen staff confirmed her statement, reporting that he'd been responsible for making the coffee and bringing it to her, whereupon the two had stood around and chatted for a good ten minutes about what had happened while she drank it. When he'd returned to collect her tray, she'd still been sitting there like she'd never moved, reading the paper.

As fruitless interview followed fruitless interview, Casey was beginning to wonder if whoever had killed Alicia Nunn had come dressed in Harry Potter's invisibility cloak. But then, just as they were about to wrap it up, one of the groundsmen had mentioned that the young boy who'd been helping him collect some golf balls that had overshot the golf course that day would like to have a word. 'Said he saw someone,' he said. 'A woman. Said I should have seen her too, since we were both standing in the same place. Except I keeps my eye on my work. Unlike him.' He made no attempt to conceal his disapproval.

'Well,' said Casey brightly, 'maybe it's an ill wind this time.'

As the young boy in question was duly ushered forth, Casey began to get excited. Maybe Justin Smith, which was how he introduced himself, held the key to this whole mystery.

'I never wanted to say nothing,' he said, speaking into his chest, his shoulders hunched and his fists shoved into the pockets of his oversized hoody. 'They was miles away.'

'Your boss said you told him it was a woman.'

'Yeah. Might 'ave been. They was on a bike. A bit wobbly. And with a basket on the front, I think. Men don't usually have baskets, do they? They're a bit, y'know . . . '

'Girly?'

49

Justin had the grace to look embarrassed.

'That's a very good observation, Justin,' Casey said encouragingly. *Though you could do with a lesson on gender stereotyping*, she would have liked to add.

Justin raised his head from his chest and looked suddenly rather pleased with himself. 'Thanks,' he said, although it sounded more like *fanx* to Casey's ears. 'I think it must have been the basket that put it into my head in the first place. That the cyclist was a woman, I mean. They was just a blur, really.' His head returned to his chest. 'Sorry I can't say no more. But I can't make stuff up, can I?'

Casey smiled. Despite everything, she liked Justin. He was a lot more observant than some police officers she knew. 'You've been very helpful, Justin,' she said. 'Very helpful indeed.'

Jody, at the wheel again as they finally headed back into Brockhaven, looked rather pleased with herself too. Justin's evidence backed up her own suspicions — that the bicycle key she'd discovered might well be relevant to the case.

It was only fair, Casey said, that Jody should follow her sharp nose with this one. There were two or three bike shops in Brockhaven and its environs. It was a long shot, but maybe someone who worked in one of these places might recognise the kind of lock this key came from — might even remember who they'd sold it to. Casey had been pessimistic about the chances of that happening earlier. But their luck had changed for the better once Jason Smith had turned up. Maybe they were on a roll at last.

'What are you going to be doing, boss?' Jody asked.

'Me? I'm going to be doing a bit of thinking back at the station,' she replied wearily. 'I need to find out who that married lover is for one thing. Somebody must know.'

'For someone with a name that sounds just like *nun*, she doesn't sound much like one, does she, boss?'

Casey smiled. 'That's quite funny, Jody,' she said. *For you*, she added mentally as she climbed out of the car.

51

* * *

'Hard day, Inspector?' the duty sergeant said as she swung by his desk. 'Must be something in the air. I saw PC Carter fifteen minutes ago heading for the canteen. She looked even more knackered than you.'

Gail? Here? Wasn't she supposed to be out at the Nunns' place? 'Cheers, Noakesy. I was just heading there myself actually,' she said.

'Keep away from the shepherd's pie. That's all I'm saying,' he called after her as she continued on her way.

'I'll bear that in mind, Sergeant Noakes,' she replied.

* * *

Gail Carter was making her way through a huge baguette at a small table in a secluded part of the canteen. 'Gail! Hi! I'll be right over,' Casey called out. 'Let me place my order first.'

Eliciting a promise from Tracey behind the counter that she'd bring her the grub and the coffee as soon as it was ready, she joined her friend. 'I've ordered sausage, egg and chips,' she said, pulling a grim face. 'I know, but honestly I can't do this investigation on lettuce.'

'Well, I'm hardly one to give lectures on nutrition,' Gail said through her half-eaten baguette. 'Never mind. If we go to three aerobics sessions next week instead of two we'll work it off.'

Casey grinned. It was a noble idea, though whether it would actually happen was an entirely different thing. 'Noaksey said you were here. So what happened with the Nunns?'

'They don't want me,' Gail said. 'Said God was all the support they needed, thank you very much.'

'Hard to compete with him,' Casey teased.

Gail, deep in thought, didn't react to Casey's remark. 'They're an odd couple,' she said. 'The way they act makes me think they'd prefer to put the whole sorry episode behind them. It's like Alicia's just an embarrassment to them.'

Casey agreed it certainly sounded that way.

'Whatever your kid's done — and having an affair with a married man isn't the worst thing in the world — you wouldn't think they'd bear a grudge beyond the grave, would you? Not towards your own daughter.'

'This affair. It's niggling me, I'll be honest,' Casey said. 'It wouldn't be the first time a mistress decided she'd had enough of being someone's bit on the side. What if she asked him to come and see her at the manor? Gave him an ultimatum?'

'It's a thought,' Gail said. 'He gets a phone call. She tells him the game's up. They meet at the tower because no one ever goes up there in the winter months. Then — poof! — he tips her over the edge.'

'If only we knew his name.'

'Lorraine might,' Gail said.

'The sister?'

'I think we should pay her a visit.'

'What, now? What about your carb-fest?'

54

But Casey was already on her feet. 'It'll wait,' she said.

★ ★ ★

Lorraine Nunn ran a stall at Brockhaven market that sold flowers, Gail informed her as they walked the short distance from the station to the centre of the village. Today was Wednesday, so she'd be there.

'Tell me about Alicia's sister,' Casey said.

'Half-sister actually,' Gail said. 'From the father's first marriage.'

'How's she bearing up?'

'Well, I haven't seen much of her. I think she keeps her distance from her parents just like her sister did,' Gail said.

Up ahead Casey caught her first glimpse of the market. 'Well, let's hope Alicia was as indiscreet as she was unfortunate and she let the lover's name slip,' she said grimly.

Business wasn't exactly booming at Lorraine Nunn's flower stall. Lorraine, dressed in jeans, boots and jumper with

55

the extra layer of a quilted jacket to keep out the cold, alternately rubbed her hands together and blew on her fingers. She had the kind of ruddy, broken-veined complexion that people who worked in the open often possessed, and her wind-tossed shoulder-length hair looked in need of some serious pampering. Casey would have said she was a good twenty years older than her sister from photos she'd seen, but maybe that was because Alicia had been nothing if not well-groomed.

Gail greeted her as if she were an old friend. Lorraine, however, took a moment to recognise her. It was a shock, Casey realised, when she finally did.

'What's happened?' Lorraine asked, stumbling over her words. 'Is it about Alicia?'

'It's all right, Lorraine,' Gail said. 'We've just come to have a word. This is Detective Inspector Clunes.'

Casey felt herself to be suddenly under scrutiny. Lorraine Nunn had none of the ready charm of her half-sister, that was for sure. Over the phone Alicia had come across as bubbly and well-spoken — someone who would fit into any social situation. Not so Lorraine. Daughter from the father's first marriage, Gail had said. Who did she take after — him, or the deceased mother?

Not wishing to be rebuffed, Casey didn't even try to make an impression on the woman, merely greeting her with a nod of the head. 'Apparently you told Gail that your sister was having an affair,' she said.

Lorraine nodded. A glimmer of understanding began to dawn. 'You want me to tell you who it was with, do you?'

'Do you know?'

She gave a cackle of amusement. 'I should say I do. Never stopped talking about him. Andy something. Worked up at Draper's. One of the big cheeses. Finance director, something like that. Big house up the top end of Brockhaven Road.'

'Thank you, Lorraine. That's very useful,' Gail said.

Casey was already on her iPhone trying to catch some wifi so she could get on

Draper's website. How many finance directors named Andy could one company have? she asked herself as, with one last cheerful wave to Lorraine, she strode on ahead.

★　★　★

'I'm sorry, but Mr King has had to go home.' The receptionist sounded desperately apologetic. 'His secretary tried to contact you but you left no number.' She pushed a yellow Post-it note toward Casey. A quick glance revealed it to be Andy King's home address. 'His wife rang him, apparently. Something to do with pranging her car. He left right away.'

'Right. Thanks. You've been very helpful.'

'Do you want this?' The receptionist held the Post-it note between an elegantly manicured and painted thumb and forefinger.

'It's all right. I've already memorised it,' Casey replied, already halfway towards the exit. Highgate Hall, Brockhaven

Road, Brockhaven. It was hardly rocket science.

★　★　★

It was the silver fox himself who opened the door to Casey. He was still in his smart work suit, but he'd removed the tie, and the top button of his shirt was undone. From the unruly state of his hair, he appeared to have been running his fingers through it. Either that or someone else had. *No, don't go there*, Casey sternly told herself. His smile was polite, but behind his glasses Casey saw apprehension. So, he *did* have something to worry about, then.

'Mr King. I hope it's still convenient to talk to you.' She flashed her ID at him and stood firm, just in case he thought she was giving him an option.

'This must be about the events up at Oakham Manor.' He cast a nervous glance upstairs.

'The murder of Alicia Nunn.' No point in beating about the bush.

'You'd better come inside.' He stood

59

back to allow her in.

A glance at the oyster-coloured walls and the gleaming polished wood floor in the wide hallway told Casey all she needed to know about the married life of the Kings. It looked enviable, but there was a sterility about these elegant surroundings that made Casey consider with a sudden burst of sentimental fondness her own messy house with its scuffed paintwork and toys scattered everywhere.

He was terribly sorry about all this, he said. Soon after Casey's call to his office to say she was on her way, his wife had rung him, distraught. She'd pranged her new car driving it out of the garage, he said, repeating what Casey already knew.

'Pre-wedding nerves,' he went on, continuing to glance repeatedly upstairs as he spoke, to where Casey gathered his 'distraught' wife must have taken herself off in order to recover from her accident.

'And now with everything that's happened at Oakham Manor, there are more problems. It's a dilemma, actually, to know whether to pull out of hosting the wedding there at all,' he said, manfully keeping up the patter like someone afraid of silence. 'I said leave it a while, but Maddy refuses. She was off to look at another venue earlier, in fact. But she didn't even get as far as the bottom of the drive.'

Tragic, thought Casey. *Meanwhile, Alicia Nunn gets pushed off the top of a tower and falls to her death. There is no justice in this world.*

'I insisted she go for a lie-down and take a couple of her pills to calm her nerves. Poor Maddy's got a lot on her mind — mother of the bride, you know how it is.'

Casey didn't. She'd always thought it was the bride who was supposed to go a bit crazy. Didn't people talk about Bridezilla?

'Mr King, I need to ask you a personal question.' He'd never shut up unless she shut him up, she decided.

'Yes. Yes, of course. But let's go into the living room.'

The living room was just as sterile as the hall, Casey thought. Although she might have be reading too much into it — what she knew about interior design you could write on the back of the Post-it note that had Andy King's expensive address scrawled on it.

'My wife knows nothing about my affair with Alicia,' he said once they were inside and he'd shut the door firmly behind them. 'I beg you, please — you mustn't involve her in this.' His head hung low, like a man who suspected he might be destined for the noose. Well, you had to admire him for his honesty at least. Or was he playing the long game? Readily admitting to one offence — that of adultery — in the hope it might get him off the hook for another much more serious one that might end in a life sentence?

'I'm not here to pass judgement,' Casey said. 'But Alicia Nunn's death wasn't suicide. Someone is responsible and it's my job to find out who.'

'I don't know how you got to me, but Brockhaven's a small place. I suppose it was only a matter of time,' he said. 'Given the nature of our relationship, it's hardly surprising I'm in the frame.'

'You're not in the frame. Or at least not necessarily,' Casey said. 'You may well have a cast-iron alibi for the day of her murder.'

'The thing is, Inspector, I don't,' he said. 'In fact, on the morning of Alicia's murder I walked over to see her. I wanted to tell her it was all over between us.'

Well, well, well. How very inconvenient for you, Casey thought, not without some glee. 'So, tell me the nature of your relationship with the deceased.'

Casey heard her phone ringing from the depths of her bag. Without taking her eyes from Andy King's face, she groped her way to the off button. She didn't want to miss one single flicker of his eyes.

'Alicia and I first got together two years ago,' he began. 'I'd seen her about the place — Draper's, where we both worked — and I was attracted to her right away. It soon became clear the feeling was mutual. Before we knew it we were knee-deep in the throes of an affair. She lived at home at the time. Though things had been difficult for a long while with

63

her father. There was a lot of religion flying around — Old Testament stuff, she used to say. Anyway, they found out about us somehow.' He seemed to be deliberating whether or not to go on. Casey waited. 'There was a huge row, she said. It shook her up badly. She told me that if her mother hadn't restrained her father, then . . . ' He left the sentence unfinished, leaving Casey to draw her own conclusions.

Note to self, she thought. *Pay the Nunns a visit at the very next opportunity. Second note to self: he could be lying to put me off the scent.*

'You loved her but you planned to tell her your affair was over?'

'Over for the second time, actually,' he said. 'The first time *she* was the one to end it. Right out of the blue. Said she'd got a new job and it came with a place to live, which meant there was no need to stay at home anymore. Wouldn't tell me where. Said it was better that way. I tried her phone but she'd changed the number.'

'So how did things start up again?'

'A couple of months ago, Lisa — my

daughter — asked Maddy and me to go along with them to a pre-wedding tasting at Oakham Manor, to finalise the dishes and the wines for the wedding.'

'And of course Alicia would have been there, hosting the event,' Casey said.

He nodded. 'It was awkward. You can imagine. I hardly said a thing all night. Hardly tasted a thing either.'

Once home he struggled with his desire to ring her now he knew where to find her again, he said. And he resisted too. For one whole week. But then he could resist no longer. He rang her. They agreed to meet. Within days they were back to square one.

'Tell me what happened when you went to Oakham Manor the day Alicia died.' For a moment Casey wondered if he were about to cry. But no, he was simply gathering himself. It was a long story and he wanted to get the bits in the right order, he said. He'd been awake all the previous night, he told her, thinking about what to do.

'You did have a conscience about it, then?'

65

'Not as much as I should. Truth was, I didn't end it through conscience. I ended it because I was a coward. I was scared of Maddy or Lisa finding out.' That was honest. 'I imagined being dis-invited to my daughter's wedding, excluded from her life and from the lives of any future grandchildren too,' he said. 'Next morning, I slept in. When I finally got up, I told Maddy I was off to work and walked all the way to the manor house.'

'Why walk? Why not take your car?' To avoid being seen by a witness? She'd seen his car out front. It wasn't one you'd forget easily.

He'd needed the time to plan exactly what he was going to say, he said. If he'd driven he'd have arrived too soon.

'What time did you arrive there?'

'About half ten, eleven o'clock,' he said.

'Did you go straight to reception?'

'No. I'd texted Alicia when I was halfway there to check it was okay. She texted back. Said to meet me at the top of the tower. It would be more private there, she said.'

Hell, yes, thought Casey. *Nice and private for a murder.* Did she get angry when he told her it was over? Threaten to tell his wife? His daughter? Did she taunt him with her phone? The phone they still hadn't found? Wave it around in front of him; remind him she had their numbers? *Hands-on* was how Kathy Ling had described her. Always keen to keep her clients up to speed with events. Was that when he ended her life, as well as their affair?

'When I rang her she sounded just the same as she always did — warm, eager to talk, looking forward to seeing me,' he went on. 'But when I got to the top of the tower she'd changed. She seemed nervous.'

'Did she suspect why you were coming to see her, do you think?'

'I don't know how she can have,' said King. 'I gave nothing away in my telephone call.'

She'd told him that she could only give him five minutes, he said. She was expecting someone. And she couldn't risk the two of them being seen together.

Should she believe him? Casey wondered. It was tempting.

'It was like she was willing me to go away,' he said. 'I felt rushed. Couldn't think straight or say what I'd planned. It was like she was looking over her shoulder all the time, barely listening.' In the end, he said, he'd funked it. Told her he wouldn't bother her if she were busy. Then he kissed her — perfunctorily, since she almost pushed him away — and left.

'And that was the last time I saw her alive,' he said. 'That's the truth, Inspector. I'll swear that in a court of law.'

'Come with me to the station right now then. Give a DNA sample. You can clear your name in no time. If you're innocent.'

His expression suggested this was a request he was reluctant to comply with. Just as she'd started to believe in his innocence too. Now the doubts she'd held at bay returned. What if this were just a yarn? What if the murderer were sitting right in front of her?

'If you've got nothing to fear you'll come with me,' Casey said.

He glanced upwards, nervously. Ah, the

wife. Upstairs, blissed out on whatever tablets she took to calm her nerves after her stressful incident with the car.

'Do I have to come right now?'

'I have no evidence to make an arrest, Mr King,' Casey said. 'But if you don't comply with my request before twenty-four hours have elapsed, I'll be paying another visit.'

'Thank you.' Relief shone from his eyes.

'That gives you time enough to explain a few things to your wife,' she said. Just in case he imagined he was in the clear.

Outside she checked her phone. Two missed calls now, one from Dom and one from Jody. Dom would have to wait.

'Jody,' she said.

'I've been to every bike shop in the vicinity,' Jody said. 'No luck.'

'Never mind. You tried.' Casey felt an unexpected burst of affection towards her younger colleague.

'Thanks. So what have you been up to?'

Casey quickly filled her in.

'Did he do it?' Jody wanted to know.

'I'd say no, but I need to keep an eye

on him,' Casey said. 'Make sure he comes down to the station as he promised. If he doesn't . . . well, I might have to go and fetch him next time.'

'And I'll go through the new forensics report that's just come in.' You had to admire Jody's dogged approach to solving this crime, Casey thought. 'Good idea,' she said. 'Ring me if you get anything.'

It was a spur-of-the-moment thing to ring Gail. She knew the Nunns' routine best and she'd already made a few interesting observations about their reaction to their daughter's death. Maybe she could answer a simple question. If Mr Nunn had murdered his own daughter, or — which was more likely given the nature of their relationship — lost his temper with her and accidentally killed her, then how he had got to and from Oakham Manor?

'Gail, I was thinking of popping in on the Nunns. I need some information first though. Do you know if they possess a ladies' bike?'

'A bike? Why do you want to know?'

Before she could get further than describing what Jason Smith had seen from the golf course on that day, Gail interrupted her.

'I can't see Mrs Nunn on a bike, Case,' she said, sounding amused. 'She's extremely overweight, not to mention unfit. She might make it to the top of the street but she'd be out of breath if she tried to get any further.'

'Let me finish. What I'm saying is this. Jason made the assumption a woman was riding it because it was a woman's bike. He said it had one of those big old-fashioned wicker baskets at the front. But he was too far away to see the person riding it properly. It could have been a man.'

'Well, I . . . '

Now it was Casey's turn to interrupt. She needed to get it all out while it was still bubbling away in her head. 'What if Mr Nunn had heard that the affair was on again? What if, in his fury, he borrowed his wife's bike and rode out to the tower to confront her?'

There was a pause. 'That's good,

Casey,' Gail said. 'Except there's just one problem.'

'What?'

'Mr Nunn might have ridden a bike at one time, but he's barely able to walk up the stairs these days, let alone take a three-mile round cycle trip and climb — how many steps to the top of the folly tower? He's waiting for a hip replacement operation, Casey.'

★ ★ ★

So it was back to the drawing board. What to do now? Should she go and see the Nunns anyway, just in case Mr Nunn was pulling the wool over Gail's eyes? If she nipped round the back and peeped through the kitchen window, would she catch him doing the samba with Mrs Nunn? No, even she could see this was ridiculous.

Her phone bleeped a message. Dom again. She left it. It rang a second time. Gail was back.

'No,' she said. 'They haven't got a bike.'

'How do you know?' Casey said.

'Because I'm *here*, aren't I? At the Nunns'.'

'You never said.'

'You didn't give me a chance.'

There may have been some truth in this. 'Sorry,' she mumbled. 'Too busy putting forward my barking mad theory.'

'I've looked in the garage and up the side passage. Nothing. Then, just as I was thinking that if it were me and I'd used it as my method of transport to commit a murder, I'd dump it, the district nurse got out of her car, which was a huge stroke of luck. I asked her if she'd ever seen either of the Nunns on a bike and she said certainly not. Neither of them is in any shape to do any exercise other than chair-based ones, what with Mr Nunn's hip and Mrs Nunn's bad legs.'

Casey's phone beeped a signal that another text message was coming through. It could have been Jody. She may have got something.

'And then she said something very interesting . . . '

'Gail, I've got to go. I keep getting messages.'

'Yes, but wait a minute . . . '

It was too late. Casey had already cut the call. She glanced at her phone. A missed call plus a text message from Dom. She couldn't really ignore him in favour of Jody. It might be to do with Finlay.

'At last!'

'Is Finlay okay?' Casey asked.

'As far as I know,' Dom said. 'He's at playgroup. Listen, Casey. This might be important. I just got back from the market. I bought masses of daffs because they were going cheap. I thought, why not, you can never have enough fl — '

'Dom, is that why you rang me? To give me a rundown of how you spent your day? I'm trying to solve a murder investigation here!'

There was a pause while Dom took a big breath. 'Casey, this *is* about the murder investigation. But if I hadn't been to the flower stall, it wouldn't have triggered my memory of driving back from Oakham Manor on the day that

Alicia Nunn was murdered.'

She froze. 'Go on.'

His car been the only one on the road, he said. He'd already told her that when she'd asked him for anything he could remember. He'd never known the road so quiet was what he'd said, remember? Yes, yes, go on, she said. He'd been drawn by the special offer on daffodils at the flower stall on the market — five bunches for a pound, if she was interested — *she wasn't* — and that was when his memory was triggered.

'The woman on the stall was the woman I'd seen on a bike heading to Oakham Manor when I was on my way back.'

Lorraine Nunn. Oh, joy!

'Are you absolutely sure?' she said. 'Describe her.'

He did. There was no mistake. 'Does this mean I no longer have to submit a sample of my DNA?' Dom was terrified of being on any official file. No one was safe from Big Brother these days, he insisted.

'You'll have to ask Jody, Dom,' Casey

teased. 'She's still got her eye on you, you know.' Speaking of Jody . . . 'Look, love, this is really brilliant, but I need to make another call.'

'OK then, now I've solved your case for you, I will detain you no longer.'

Damn cheek! She hung up.

'Jody, have you got something big for me? Because I've got something huge for you.'

'You first,' Jody said.

Casey reported everything Dom had said at breakneck speed.

'Boy, oh boy,' Jody said when she'd finished. 'You'll like this then. Traces of pollen from a number of flowers were found at the scene. From flowers not native to the British climes.'

'Lorraine Nunn sells imported flowers on her stall,' Casey said. She had another sudden thought. 'It's just occurred to me,' she added. 'I think you've been asking the wrong question at the bike shops. Instead of asking did anyone know which lock might fit the key, perhaps you should have been asking if anyone had been in to buy a new lock for their bike recently.'

A pause, then, 'Of course. If she's a regular cyclist then she can't afford to be without her lock. I'm onto it, boss. Right now.'

Another text had arrived from Gail while they'd been talking. Casey read it with a rush of excitement. *Before you cut me off I was going to say the nurse said the only bike she'd seen at the house was Lorraine's*, it said.

Nice one, Gail, she texted back. She was looking forward to having a good chat with Lorraine Nunn.

* * *

'I didn't do it, you know. I wasn't even there.'

It was late; they'd had to wait hours for the solicitor to turn up. Lorraine Nunn knew her rights. But she was bluffing. There was too much evidence stacked against her. Though much of it was circumstantial — Alicia's phone found in one of Lorraine's kitchen drawers, for example — there was one piece of evidence that Casey knew would nail it.

'She must have left it at mine,' Lorraine said.

'Then how do you explain this text message received by Alicia on the morning of her death and sent on your phone?' Casey read it exactly as it had been transcribed. '*You told me it was in the bag. On way. You owe me an explanation.*'

Lorraine glanced at her solicitor. He gave her a look that suggested she keep it zipped.

'Do you ride a bike, Miss Nunn?'

The solicitor gave her silent permission to answer that one. 'What if I do?' she said.

Casey pushed a second bag across the table containing the bicycle key that Jody had turned up. Not two hours ago, Casey said, an officer of the law had discovered that the lady who ran the flower stall had bought a new bicycle lock from Brian's Bikes in the centre of Brockhaven.

'Could have been anybody,' Lorraine said, not unreasonably.

Except, Casey informed her, Brian's shop window looked directly out onto her

78

stall. 'He even knew your name,' she added. Lorraine sniffed. '*You told me it was in the bag.* What did you think was in the bag, Lorraine, that clearly wasn't?' Another sniff. 'I'm guessing your sister promised you something she couldn't deliver.'

There followed another long silence.

'Look, Lorraine, we can sit here all night, but is that really what you want?'

When she got no response, Casey decided it was time to move things along. She folded her hands on the table and fixed Lorraine with gimlet eyes. 'One of my officers has spoken to your bank manager. He seems to think that you were expecting an upturn in your finances. You told him that you'd been promised a big contract to do the flowers at Oakham Manor.'

'Is this true?' the solicitor hissed.

A whey-faced Lorraine nodded.

'Unfortunately, Alicia didn't have the level of authority to promise you what you so badly wanted. But she thought Robert did. She even believed she'd extracted the promise from him and texted you to that effect.'

Of course, the next day he'd remembered nothing about it. That must have been when she went ballistic at him outside the kitchen and Kathy Ling had had to break up the fight.

'Your sister had to tell you that the contract was off. You were understandably angry. Demanded to meet her to see if you could get her to change her mind.'

'No!'

'The text, Lorraine, remember?' Casey waved the bagged phone under her nose. 'I've got another piece of evidence taken from the scene here. Do you recognise this jacket?'

'Could be anyone's. Can't see much through that bag,' Lorraine said.

'Well, we happen to know it was your sister's.' It was time to bring out the big guns. 'And the handprint on the back of it is yours.'

Lorraine slumped forward in her chair. 'Okay,' she said in such a tiny voice that Casey had to strain to hear it. 'I may have pushed her. I was angry. I caught her off-balance. I didn't mean to kill her.'

80

'Before you say another word, Lorraine, I'm going to have to caution you,' she said.

* * *

'Do you think it was deliberate?'

Casey was back home at last. She'd imagined Dom would be in bed but he'd waited up for her, desperate to hear the whole story.

'She said it was an accident at first. Alicia turned her back on her. Told her she was pathetic. It must have been that which made Lorraine's blood boil,' Casey said. 'But I don't know. Some of the things she said about Alicia — well, they weren't exactly sisterly.'

'Like?'

'That she was a smug cow and her parents' favourite. And that *she'd* been the one to let the cat out of the bag about Alicia's affair with Andy King the first time. And that she was glad she had because now she wasn't the only one to disappoint her dad.'

'How do you mean?'

81

'Apparently the parents had lent Lorraine money to start her flower stall and she'd lost most of it. But compared to carrying on with a married man, that was nothing — at least not in her parents' eyes.'

Dom put his arm round Casey and drew her to him. She let out a long sigh of contentment and snuggled closer. Maybe she'd take a couple of days off at the end of the week. Spend some time with Finlay. Take him to nursery and pick him up. Go with him to feed the ducks.

'So that's that. All over. Finally, I can relax,' she sighed. She sat gazing at the flames in the artificial log fire, blissfully content.

'Er — not sure about that, Case,' Dom said. 'You see, St Mike's called.'

'About dates?'

'Right. They've had a cancellation. There's a Saturday afternoon available six weeks from now.'

Casey shrieked and almost leapt out of her warm seat. 'Six weeks? We'll never organise a wedding in six weeks!' She fixed her gaze on Dom. 'Tell me you didn't accept, Dom, please.'

He was grinning at her stupidly. Oh, why had she even asked, when she knew the answer already? He was a lost cause.

'Okay,' she said. 'It'll be a challenge. But it's do-able.' She grabbed her phone.

'Who are you ringing?' Dom asked.

'Well, I need a chief bridesmaid, don't I?' she said. 'Gail, hi. Is that you? I want to ask you a favour . . . '

The Secrets in
Their Eyes

In the ladies' room at Pitman Road Police Station, where she'd worked as a police constable for more years than she cared to remember, PC Kim Stone was attempting to disguise the shadows beneath her eyes with the help of a stick of concealer. The concealer had been a fiftieth birthday present from her two young nieces, Paris and Fay, alongside a card that had read *Age doesn't matter unless you're a cheese*, which made her chuckle every time she thought of it.

'Paris wanted to get you a book token,' Fay had declared, 'but I said you had enough books already.'

Enough books? How could anyone ever have enough books? she'd thought. Course, she would never have said so. She hoped she was a bit more tactful than her younger sister Shannon, the girls' mum, who'd had a habit since childhood of failing to engage her brain before she opened her mouth. Fortunately, neither of Kim's nieces had inherited this trait. They were both lovely girls and she was proud to call herself their aunty.

Her birthday had been three days ago, but she hadn't quite mastered how to apply the concealer yet. In fact, she looked worse now than before she'd put it on — like a panda that'd gone five rounds with a heavyweight boxer.

Shannon was good with make-up. Not that she needed it, being naturally pretty. Good with clothes too, unlike herself. In fact, Kim often thought that it was maybe her chronic lack of interest in what she put on her back that had made her choice of profession so easy. You knew where you were with a uniform.

Dad hadn't bought her anything, of course. Without Mum around to remind him of important dates anymore, birthdays just slipped his mind these days. It would have been nice, though, if Shannon had thought to do what she herself had started to do for Shannon and the girls — buy something with her own money and pretend it was from him. But that would never have occurred to her.

It wouldn't have occurred to her to invite Dad to move in with her either, even though she had the room now she'd kicked Ray out. In the end, when it became clear Dad wasn't managing without Mum, it was Kim who'd been the one to sell her flat and move back into her childhood home. Now she was back in the same bedroom she'd shared with Shannon as a girl, while Dad snored through the night in the master bedroom next door. It was the snoring that was causing the shadows under her eyes. That, and being at his constant beck and call.

Just as she was in the middle of remembering that today was the day the fishmonger called at the house, and she really ought to ring Dad to make sure he kept an ear out for him when he knocked or there'd be nothing for tea, the door to the ladies' opened and DC Janice Masters came in. Kim put her domestic concerns to the back of her mind.

'Wondered if you'd be in here. The Super's looking for you,' Janice said. 'You know what it'll be, don't you?'

Kim experienced a sudden flutter of nerves. 'The FLO results,' she said. 'Oh dear! I've failed. I just know it.'

'Don't be daft,' Janice said. 'You'll have walked it. If anybody would make a great family liaison officer, it's you.'

'Thanks, but you're just saying that.'

'No, I'm serious. You're perfect for it. Non-threatening, unflappable, and a good listener too.' She waggled her finger at Kim. 'Trouble with you, my girl, is you don't know your own worth. Now, pull your shoulders back and get in there.'

Kim smiled. Janice was only thirty, and a DC already, ambitious and single-minded. She'd probably been giving herself pep talks ever since she first learned to speak. Mum had given the best pep talks when she was alive. It was reassuring to think that there was another person in Kim's life now who was just as willing and able to give her a kick in the pants when she needed it most.

'Thanks, Janice,' she said. 'I appreciate it.'

'So you should,' Janice said. 'But before you go . . . ' She raised her hand to her face and made a rubbing-in gesture.

'I've overdone it, haven't I?' Furiously, Kim dabbed away at her cheeks.

'Well, maybe. Just a bit.'

★ ★ ★

There was something of the zealot about Superintendent Chris Cleaver. The squad was her life — everyone said so — and nothing else mattered. On her desk there were no family photos, or any other personal touches in the room. Kim had worked under the Super for five years now. But try as she might, she could find no clue as to the kind of person she was when she wasn't at work. As a rule she was intimidating, sharp, and brutally to the point, with little time for small talk. But as a nervous Kim took the seat that was indicated, she didn't think she she'd imagined the ghost of a smile that flickered over the Super's face this afternoon.

'Congratulations, Kim,' she said. 'You're now a fully qualified family liaison officer.'

Kim felt like punching the air victoriously. But that wasn't the sort of thing you did in front of the Super. She contented herself with a smile and a *thank you, ma'am*.

'So, how do you feel about starting immediately in your new role?' The Super fixed Kim with her steely gaze.

'What — today, you mean? I — well — yes. Of course.' Excitement buzzed inside her like a hive of bees. 'What's the case?'

'A missing woman. I've just had an investigation room set up. Walk with me and I'll fill you in on the details en route.'

Kim jumped up immediately. You didn't dawdle when you were with the Super. Funny how the exhaustion she'd felt earlier suddenly seemed to have completely evaporated. Right now she was raring to go.

★ ★ ★

In the rapidly put-together investigation room, the Super addressed the small team. Janice was already there. And young Alan. John Farmer too, and a couple more officers she recognised. These were hard times in policing and officers were being spread thinly, the Super announced apologetically. 'So we'll all have to work twice as hard,' she said. Her words were greeted with a collective groan. 'Working particularly hard will be PC Stone, whom I've appointed as the FLO.'

There was a ripple of approval around the table. Someone even broke into applause. Kim wriggled in her chair, hating the attention. Fortunately it didn't last long. The Super was speaking again. Quickly she summarised the events as they'd so far occurred. 'Family name is Feaver,' she said. 'Live in Orston. Mother's name, Adele; father, Adam. There are two children: daughter Eloise, nineteen, in her gap year; and son in his early twenties, out of work, name of Emerson. All clear so far?'

Everyone nodded. On she sped. 'The daughter goes away for the weekend,' she continued. 'Comes back Monday morning. No mum. Neither her father nor her brother can help her out as to when they'd last seen her. Brother's been out partying every night. Hasn't been home.'

Kim scribbled away furiously. Her role as FLO was not to be part of the investigation team but to support the family. But the more familiar she was with the details, the easier it would be for her to keep the family up to speed with how the investigation was going.

'Adam Feaver maintains he's been holed up in his study all weekend. Thinks he's seen Adele down the garden on the Sunday but he couldn't swear whether it was morning or afternoon. He's a writer, apparently. Loses track of time when he's in the middle of a novel, apparently.'

Adam Feaver! Of course! As soon as she'd mentioned the name Kim knew she'd heard it before. But only now did she remember. Last time she'd been to the library to change Dad's books and grab one for herself, there'd been a display of his novels at the front desk. She'd leafed through one of the books and seen his picture. Now she came to think of it, under the photograph were the

words *photo by Adele Feaver.*

'They report her missing when they get a call later on Monday morning from the sixth form college where she works. Adele Feaver hasn't turned up and has failed to call in sick. It's a mystery, especially as Monday's apparently the first day of the art department's summer exhibition and Mrs Feaver's the curator.'

Alan Togher raised his hand, catching the Super's attention immediately. Kim liked the boy very much — she'd puppy-walked him when he'd first joined the force, and to this day he still followed her around eagerly; her own personal lap dog was how Janice described him. What's a curator? he wanted to know. Patiently the Super explained it meant someone in charge of — in this case — an art exhibition.

'Don't ever be afraid to ask questions, Alan,' she added, picking up on the expressions of disdain on the faces of some of the more experienced officers. 'It's only by asking questions that we get the answers.'

Alan looked chuffed. He'd go far, that

one, Kim was convinced.

'Anyway, according to the daughter, she'd never have missed it for the world. It was her favourite time of the year.'

'So what now, ma'am?' Janice asked.

'What now is this. Three days have passed, and there's still no sign of Adele Feaver, and she's not picking up her mobile. So we're duty-bound to report her to the missing persons bureau, enter her details on the PNC for circulation nationwide, and check out any CCTV. That's just for starters.'

'House to house?' Janice enquired.

The Super nodded. 'A check of local hospital admissions, checks on her computer, and with her bank too, of course.'

'Work colleagues? They'll need talking to too, won't they?' John Farmer asked.

The Super agreed. 'Sooner or later, of course,' she added, 'if we don't find her we're going to have to apply for her dental and medical records as well as search the house.' She glanced at Kim. 'That might be a sensitive area, Kim. You need to let them know why we're doing it — that they're not under suspicion, but that there may be some personal information somewhere in the house they've missed that could help.'

Kim nodded. 'Is there any reason to believe the family will stand in the way of a search?' she asked.

'Well, they're not that thrilled that we're only now taking her disappearance seriously,' the Super said. 'Even when I explained that by law three days must be allowed to elapse before an adult who disappears from their place of residence can be termed 'missing'. Unless they're deemed to be at risk, which she wasn't till today, of course.'

With a glance at the wall clock, the Super said they'd done enough talking and now it was time to start doing. She'd leave it to John Farmer to apportion the various roles, she added. 'Except Janice. I want you to interview the family again, more closely this time. And Kim, you need to go with her and make yourself known.'

'Yes, ma'am.' She couldn't wait.

★　★　★

How lovely it would be to live in such a picturesque village, Kim remarked from the driving seat to Janice as they entered the picturesque village of Orston. It had everything — a lovely old church, a village green, a war memorial. Why, there was even a tearoom, she said.

'Bit boring though after a bit, wouldn't you say?' Janice remarked. 'Some of us would rather go clubbing.'

Kim laughed. She didn't want to say it, but she'd never actually been to a club — though of course, in her day they were still called discos. She'd never liked crowds, but always preferred quiet places. Which reminded her.

'This Adam Feaver,' she said. 'It's such a coincidence.' Briefly she filled Janice in about her visit to the library and the display of his novels that she'd seen there. 'Michael, the librarian, said he'd booked him to come and give a talk, sometime this week I believe. Asked me if I'd thought about coming.'

'Michael, eh?' There was a teasing note in Janice's voice.

Kim flushed. 'It's not like that. I've

known him ages,' she said. 'Hardly surprising, as I spend so much time there.'

'Sounds like he was asking you for a date.' Janice widened her eyes teasingly.

'Honestly, Janice, what are you like? I think he was just desperate to make sure he had an audience.'

'Trust me, he was asking because he fancies you, not because he wanted bums on seats.'

Could she be right? Thinking back, he had seemed quite disappointed when she said she didn't think she'd be able to come because she didn't like leaving Dad in the evenings when she'd been on duty all day.

'Anyway, it doesn't matter now,' she said with a wistful note in her voice. 'I don't suppose he'll be giving the talk anyway.'

★　★　★

'So what's your first impression of the Feaver clan?' Janice asked as they strolled down the driveway away from the large grey house back to the car.

'They're obviously distraught,' Kim said. 'Even if they're not all showing it the same way. The boy, Emerson, didn't say much at all.'

'You haven't met my brother,' Janice said. 'Believe me, Emerson's a chatterbox in comparison.'

'Eloise, on the other hand ... She wouldn't shut up. Kept going over and over the story. How she'd got in late and assumed everyone was in bed except her brother, because no one ever knows where he is,' said Kim.

'Not much love lost between those two, d'you think?'

Kim, not wanting to get into a discussion about sibling rivalry, steered the topic back to the main one. 'Then all that stuff about how she knew there must be something up next morning when her mother wasn't down for breakfast, and how she'd sent her dad to wake her up because she knew Adele would be needed at college.'

'He — Adam — is blaming himself, I think,' Kim said. 'If he'd only gone to bed instead of falling asleep at his computer.'

'Funny how you can share a house with three other people and not know where they are.'

'Well, it is a big place,' Kim said enviously. Thinking about the Feavers' large place and how it compared to the little box she shared with Dad sent her spinning right back into the domestic realm again. 'Damn,' she squealed. They were in the car now and she'd already started the engine. 'I need to make a call to my dad, Janice. Can you hang on a mo?'

'I'm in no hurry,' Janice said.

Kim threw her a grateful glance and hurriedly switched off the engine. A quick time check suggested the fishmonger may already have been and gone, and if Dad had been dozing in his chair — a habit that was becoming more and more entrenched these days — he'd never have heard the knock on the door. But if luck were on her side, she might just catch him.

He picked up just as the call was about to go to voicemail.

'Dad, how you doing?'

'Kim, is that you, love?'

'Who you expecting? The Queen?'

Jollying him up had become a habit since Mum died. It was Kim's way of steering him away from dwelling on all the small grievances that had built up in his head during the day, before they became one big one. Not to mention her particular way of keeping her own resentment hidden. One of these days she feared she might just come out and say that yes, it was awful for him, he'd lost his wife — but she'd lost her mother. What about *her* feelings? She never would, of course. Who knew what kind of a Pandora's box might result.

'Well, I hoped Shannon would call. Or one of the neighbours. No one's been near all day.'

Kim couldn't bear to hear the frailty in her father's voice. It was heartbreaking and infuriating. How was it possible to feel two almost opposite emotions both at the same time? If you were to believe half the stuff you saw on TV and read in stories about families, you'd think they were the greatest thing since sliced bread. She couldn't be the only person in the world to feel such confusion, surely?

'Nobody's been?' she said. 'What, not even the fishmonger?'

'What fishmonger? I wasn't expecting any fishmonger.'

It was just as she feared. Oh, well, no use berating him about it. What was done was done.

'No worries,' she said, irritating even herself with her cheerfulness. 'I'll stop off somewhere and get something for tea.' She had a vague idea there was a village shop in Orston. Perhaps she'd be able to pick up some fish fingers as a substitute for the fresh haddock she'd been pinning her hopes on, she mused, as she rang off.

'Still playing up, is he?'

Just occasionally she wished she didn't use Janice as a sounding bag. She smiled wanly, shrugging her shoulders, refusing to be drawn.

'It's complicated,' she said. 'Now where's ye olde village shop?'

★   ★   ★

Kim had filled her wire basket with a variety of foodstuffs she thought she'd be able to assemble into an edible meal, while simultaneously completing the chores she was pretty certain Dad would only have managed to make a start on.

She took her place at the checkout behind the only other customer, a rotund woman shrouded in a black coat despite the glorious sunny day outside, who was deep in conversation with the assistant, similarly shrouded but in white nylon.

'Bold as brass she was, Brenda,' the woman said, transferring a bumper-size box of cereal from her basket onto the conveyor belt.

'They're all the same on that estate,' Brenda said, scanning the item.

'I said to her, I said, what do you think you're doing riding that round the village? Know what she said back?'

'I can imagine that whatever it was would have been peppered with language, Sandra.' With pursed lips she checked the eggs carefully for any broken ones.

'Well you're right there. It was none of my dot dot dot business, etcetera,

104

etcetera. Well, I soon put her right there. That bike belongs to a friend of mine, I said. I'd recognise it anywhere, Brenda. Well, we all would.'

Brenda nodded furiously. 'How could you not? All those plastic flowers threaded through the basket. That's Mrs Feaver's bike, all right.'

Kim felt a sudden tingle in her scalp.

'Stood there, bold as brass. Not only did she have Mrs Feaver's bike, but she was wearing one of her scarves round her neck. You know, the tie-dyes she does for the fête?'

'No! What a cheek! What did she have to say about that? That'll be twenty-eight pounds thirty-two pence, please, Sandra.'

'Excuse me!' Kim couldn't keep quiet a second longer.

The two women looked at her, immediately taking in her uniform. 'I believe you were talking about Adele Feaver?' she said.

'That's right, we was.' It was the woman called Sandra who addressed her.

'And you said someone had her bike?'

'Some girl from off the new estate. Bold as brass, loitering by the church, smoking and chatting on her mobile phone. Shouldn't be surprised if she'd stolen that from someone too, little madam!'

'Did she say where she'd found it?'

'Oh yes. Somewhere in Linton Woods. Said it was on its side with that scarf left in the basket. Said she assumed that because it wasn't locked it had been abandoned. Answer for everything, that one.'

'Is that why you're here, Officer? Has Mrs Feaver reported it missing?' Brenda put in.

An abandoned bike. A scarf left behind. She was going to have to report this right now. 'Yes,' she said. No need to tell them the truth just yet. News would get round soon enough once there'd been a press release. They needed to find this girl right now and get her to reveal exactly where she'd found Mrs Feaver's bike. There'd have to be a search. Who knew what else they might discover deep in the depths of Linton Wood.

* * *

House-to-house enquiries had located the young girl who'd found the bike in Linton Woods, but not until darkness had fallen. It had been too late to revisit the spot; so this morning at first light Kim returned, grumbling and proclaiming she was being set up, this time accompanied by the search team. She had been ordered to get herself over to the Feavers' place and wait for news.

She'd been here an hour now and still nothing, and she had no idea whether to be comforted or alarmed by the situation. The house itself seemed to be holding its breath, like it was waiting for news, in the same way they all were. Kim wandered from room to room, stopping occasionally when she found herself suddenly distracted by the sight of yet another pleasing feature — a stained-glass window, or a carved picture rail, or one more painting bearing Adele Feaver's signature, big and bold and black, stamped in the right-hand corner of each one. Only someone with an artist's eye could have imagined such a clash of colour and so many mismatching pieces of furniture and fabrics would work together so perfectly, she thought, sticking her head round the living room door just in case Adam Feaver might be there, in need of some sort of company.

He wasn't, so she quickly withdrew before the sudden urge to start plumping up cushions overtook her. Oh, what she'd give for a house like this instead of the box she shared with her dad with its flimsy doors and thin walls and narrow windows that seemed to conspire against letting in any light at all. She banished the thought immediately. She'd have to be out of her mind to want to swap places with the Feavers right now!

Pausing to straighten a picture frame en route to the kitchen, she stopped to examine its contents more carefully. The picture showed a young girl in a china-blue dress sitting upright in a hard-backed chair and stroking a ginger kitten in her lap. The lustrous blonde hair and almond-shaped blue eyes staring back at her left her in no doubt that this was Eloise, albeit a much younger Eloise than the one she'd grown familiar with over recent days.

'We don't need a policewoman in the house checking up on us and watching our every move,' *this* Eloise had insisted earlier, before stomping off upstairs, her brother trailing behind her like a docile pet.

Kim couldn't blame them really for being so hostile towards her. All she could do was gain their trust by slow degrees, the way she'd been taught on her course. Forcing her company on them would only have the opposite effect of alienating them totally.

In the kitchen the morning sunshine struck the old oak dresser at an angle, dappling the display of blue and yellow crockery with warm sunlight. There was an echo in the room of someone having only recently left; a smell of toast and coffee, crumbs on the bread board, a pot of jam with the lid off and a knife smeared with its contents. For something to do, she cleared away the breakfast debris. As she moved about the room, a tall glass vase crammed with several glorious spires of pink and purple foxgloves caught her eye. Some of the petals had dropped onto the table, so she scooped them up and tipped them in the bin.

'Oh, hello,' came a voice.

Even though she had every right to be here, Kim felt like an intruder who'd been caught red-handed snooping around in someone else's house. She stood up quickly and the bin lid clanged noisily shut.

'I was just tidying up a little,' she said as she spun round, aware of how brightly her cheeks burned.

'I should have cleared up after myself,' Adam Feaver said. 'All this time we've been married and Adele still hasn't managed to housetrain me.' He attempted a smile but it was no good. In the sunlit room he seemed a grey shadow of a man, oozing quiet desperation, as remote from the confident, smiling Adam Feaver in the photo on his book jackets as this huge farmhouse kitchen was to the little galley with its Formica tops and cupboards made from MDF that Kim shared with her dad.

'Can I do anything?' she said. 'Get you some coffee, perhaps?'

'All I seem to do is drink coffee,' he mumbled.

She thought he was turning down her offer, but he surprised her, saying that yes, a coffee would be very nice. 'Only I'll make it if you don't mind. I'm fussy when it comes to coffee.'

'Of course,' she said, relieved. One look at the fancy coffee machine had already told her that you'd need a barista's training to get the hang of that.

'You'll have one too, I hope,' he said.

Well, at least one of the Feaver family was capable of being civil. 'That would be great, thanks.'

Their eyes met briefly and she smiled warmly. It seemed to relax him. 'Look,' he said, 'I'm sorry about the kids earlier. They can be . . . well, you'll know if you've got any.'

'I have two nieces,' she said. 'They're still young but they have their moments.'

She watched him as he went about the

complicated paraphernalia of making the coffee. It was something he took great pride in, obviously. When it was ready he placed everything on a tray. 'We'll have it in my study,' he said as he picked it up. 'This way.'

She followed him across the hallway to what she surmised might very possibly be the smallest room in the house.

'I can have a cigarette in here, you see. Unless . . . ?' He threw her a questioning glance.

'Go ahead,' she said. 'It's your house, after all.'

He gestured to a battered leather chair and Kim sat down.

'No,' he said, setting the tray down on a small table, 'not really. You've seen the house. It has Adele's stamp all over it. The rest of us are consigned to our various quarters, where we can indulge in our bad taste to our hearts' content.'

She couldn't be sure if he were being serious or joking. He took a cigarette from a packet next to the tray, put it to his lips and lit it with a lighter he drew from his trouser pocket. 'She never comes in here,' he said after he'd taken a long drag. 'All this clutter makes her nervous.'

That tone again. Bitter, resentful, yet victorious too. As if he'd scored a point in some ongoing skirmish that Kim had no privy to. The room was certainly cluttered all right. Everywhere there were stacks of books, presumably because they couldn't be crammed into the already overfilled shelves that lined three walls. Against the fourth wall stood his desk with his computer and even more piles of books.

'It's hardly aesthetically pleasing.' He handed Kim her coffee. Its aroma alone made her realise just why anyone would want to go to so much trouble making it. 'But you know what they say,' he went on. 'Every writer needs a room of his own.'

'Woman,' she said, correcting him. 'Not writer. Every woman needs a room of her own. And five hundred a year.'

'A policeman who reads Virginia Woolf!' He observed her with new interest.

'Well, no,' she said. 'Not really. But everyone knows that quote.'

He smiled. 'Five hundred a year

wouldn't get you very far these days, would it?'

'I read somewhere that by today's standards five hundred would be more like twenty grand,' she said. 'So if that was just your spending money then it'd do me very nicely.'

He threw back his head and roared. His laughter transformed his face, wiping away all traces of his earlier exhaustion. She joined in too, but stopped immediately. It seemed wrong somehow to be sitting in Adam Feaver's study that smelled of books and tobacco, drinking coffee and sharing *bon mots* about a dead writer when there was a missing person to be found.

And actually, she hadn't read it in a book at all. Michael had told her this once when he'd come across her in the library one evening, where she'd been sitting in a window seat reading. It was the snooker, she'd confided. Dad had it on the TV at high volume all the time and it was driving her mad. Virginia Woolf had been right, he'd said.

When it had become apparent that she

hadn't got a clue what he was talking about he'd quoted the line, apologising for going off at a tangent about the £500. She'd told him there was absolutely no need for an apology; she'd enjoyed hearing him talk. He'd seemed pleased at that and even started to relax a little. She'd hoped he might stay to chat some more, but then he said he'd better dash, and that had been the end of that.

Thinking about Michael reminded her about the talk that Adam was meant to be giving. If she was correct, it was scheduled to take place in about three days' time. She was sure it was the last thing he needed to be reminded of right now, she said. But perhaps he ought to think about cancelling.

'Oh God, I'd forgotten all about that.' He took a final drag of his cigarette and stubbed it out in the ashtray. 'I guess I need to call them.'

'Let me do that,' she said. 'That's what I'm here for, remember. To support you and the children. I'll sort it; it won't take a minute.'

His eyes softened. 'You're very kind,' he said.

'I'm just doing my job,' she said, feeling awkward.

He couldn't know that as excuses to talk to Michael came, this was one was perfect. Funny how she'd started thinking of him more frequently since that conversation with Janice in the car yesterday. What had that girl stirred up?

A sudden sharp ring at the door jolted her out of her thoughts. A glance through the window told her there was a police car sitting outside the house.

'Oh God.' Adam had seen it too. He went suddenly limp in his seat, his cup shaking as he replaced it on the saucer.

'Why don't you take the tray back through to the kitchen?' Kim said, immediately snapping back into role. 'I'll get the door.'

'Yes,' he said, meekly. 'Thanks. I'd appreciate that.'

She didn't stay to watch him stack the tray with the coffee things, but shot out of the room and along the hall to the front door. When she opened it, Alan Togher was standing there, wearing his usual bright and eager expression.

'I thought I'd call in rather than telephone. Then I could say hello,' he said.

Alan's helmet always looked too big for him, Kim thought, not for the first time. It was as if he'd found it in a dressing-up box and was just trying it on for size.

'You'd better come in, Alan, if you have some news.' She dragged her gaze away from the helmet and back to his face again. 'Though if it's bad, perhaps you'd better tell me first.'

'Well,' he said, 'I'm not sure, to be honest. The bike and the scarf are with forensics. But because they've both been through at least one person's hands since Mrs Feaver's, we're hardly likely to learn anything from either.'

'But you've found nothing in the woods?' she asked, stepping back to allow him inside.

'No,' he said. 'Nothing at all. Though that don't mean it's not bad news. It could just mean it's not bad news *yet*.'

* ★ ★

En route home from the Feavers', Kim
called in at the library. *It's purely
business*, she told herself as she walked in
through the automatic doors. She stopped
by the notice board to compose herself
before she delivered Adam's message to
Michael.

When it became apparent that this
time, at least, the police had not arrived
bearing bad news, Adam had quickly
revived, insisting Alan stay for coffee.
Alan, as she could have predicted, had
needed no persuasion. Within in
moments he'd lifted the tense atmo-
sphere, complimenting the décor, and
commenting on the flowers in the vase
and how pretty they were and how he'd
seen some just like that in the woods.
That boy could talk the hind leg off a
donkey.

In fact the mood had got so jolly that it
had drawn the Feaver children out of
hiding. They'd quickly scurried off again,
however, once it became clear that there
was nothing to report — Eloise the first

to leave, trailing Emerson in her wake, as usual.

He was an odd young man, Emerson, Kim couldn't help thinking. Weren't boys meant to have overcome that teenage inability to join in a conversation by the time they reached his age? Or was there something else going on there? It was almost as if he couldn't quite keep up with the conversation. She'd noticed for the first time too that he had a slight limp when he walked. *Switch off,* she told herself. *You're no longer on duty, woman!*

She diverted herself by reading the notices on the board. There was a new one today, pinned up between the advert for the mothers-and-toddlers reading group and the invitation to give Nordic walking a try.

Recently widowered? Having to cook for yourself for the first time? Come and join us in the kitchen at St Anthony's Community College. Learn to cook your favourite dishes and meet new friends. Every Wednesday at 2 p.m.

If only she could persuade Dad to go to that. To say his cooking skills were basic would have been a compliment. It would have been nice to come home to a cooked meal after a hard day at work once in a while. Nothing ventured, she decided, as she tore off one of the slips at the bottom of the page bearing the contact details and slipped it into her pocket.

Unfortunately, according to the young assistant on the desk, today was Michael's day off, but she could take a message. Hiding her disappointment as best she could, Kim passed it on.

'It's no surprise really. I think he'd already resigned himself to the probability of having to cancel,' she said. 'I suppose I'd better start taking the display down.' Her sigh suggested it was more than a little inconsiderate that Adele Feaver had chosen this moment to go missing.

'Actually, while I'm here I think I might just borrow one his novels,' Kim said. Who knew, it might give her something to talk about with the author.

'Be my guest,' the assistant said begrudgingly. 'You know where they are.'

Poor Michael, Kim thought as, less

than ten minutes later, she left the library with the book tucked under her arm. She didn't envy him having to work with such a cheerful colleague day in, day out.

The rest of the evening came and went. Kim tackled the evening meal once more with as much grace as she could muster, then took herself off to bed early. The book she'd borrowed was entitled *Unforgiven*. By the time she switched off her light she'd already read about fifty pages, but so far very little had occurred.

She could see that it was beautifully written, with an economy of style and a lyricism that made it more akin to poetry than prose. But unless something happened very soon she didn't rate her chances of actually getting to the end very highly. She fell asleep with the light on, thinking of foxgloves in a glass jar. She had a strong feeling that they were significant in some way. But she was too sleepy to get her head round it right now. It would have to wait.

★ ★ ★

121

When she woke it was to Dad standing over her, a mug of tea in his hand, and the news that she'd slept through her alarm.

'Why didn't you wake me sooner?' she yelled at him, immediately regretting her words. Less than two months living back in the family home and she'd transformed into a moody teenager. Once out the shower she went to offer her apology.

'I'll make you some toast, shall I?' Dad said, which was, she knew, his way of accepting it.

It was 9.30 by the time she reached the Feavers' house. Since yesterday she was in possession of a key to the back door. That way, so Adam said, she could let herself in whenever she wanted to. *Without disturbing us* was how Kim translated this. She'd mentioned his words to Janice, when she'd rung in the previous day to make her daily report.

'I'm rubbish at this job,' Kim had said. 'I'd hoped they'd talk to me. He's friendly enough. But it's like he's just putting on a show of good manners. The kids, on the other hand, don't even bother doing that.'

'Give it time, Kim,' Janice had said. 'You've only been in the job a few days.'

It was scant comfort, Kim thought as she made her way round the back of the house. There was a woman's bicycle propped outside the back door, which was unlocked. Loud pop music was booming from the radio. Curious, she let herself in.

'Oh. Mr Feaver said you was coming. It would have been better if you'd come round the other way. I've just mopped my floor.'

Kim recognised Sandra right away, the woman she'd seen at the village shop who'd put her on to the girl who'd found the bike in Linton Woods. Today she was swathed in an overall, wearing a pair of yellow marigold gloves.

Kim was about to apologise for her thoughtlessness. But that was before she scanned the kitchen surfaces and saw how things had changed since yesterday. Everywhere was spotless. In particular, something that had been here yesterday no longer was. Something tugged at her memory. What was it she'd been thinking about just before she'd dropped off to sleep last night? Suddenly, Alan's words as he stood in the kitchen burst inside her head. *Lovely flowers, them. Funny, I just saw some like that down in the woods.*

'What have you done with them?' Kim was inside now, prowling around the kitchen, oblivious to Sandra's squeals of protest. She needed to find those damn foxgloves.

'With what?' Sandra demanded.

'Here they are!' The flowers were sticking out of the top of the bin. She made a lunge for them and retrieved them.

'I threw them out because they were dropping their petals everywhere. Never last more than a few days in water, those wild flowers,' Sandra said. 'If you ask me . . . '

Kim didn't wait to hear what else Sandra had to say on the subject of wild flowers. Without any further explanation she ran back outside, carrying the now bedraggled blooms with her, down to the bottom of the back garden. *Our garden's full of flowers*, Adam had remarked in reply to Alan's compliment yesterday. *Adele must have cut these just before she disappeared.*

Well, if she did, she certainly didn't cut them from the garden. There were no foxgloves to be seen either at the front of the house or at the back. She was going to have to get these specimens to the investigation team to see if they could identify where they'd come from. Linton Woods would be her guess.

And if they had? How had they got to the house? Kim juggled every explanation she could think of. The simplest was that Adele had picked the flowers a couple of days before she'd gone missing. But if that were the case they'd surely have been dead by now, and yesterday they still looked good. And what had Sandra said about wild flowers never lasting long in water? She was pretty sure that was the case from her own experience too.

There were two other explanations, both equally intriguing. Adele's bike was still in the woods, so the only way she could have brought the flowers back to the house was if someone had given her a lift home, suggesting she return later to pick up the bike — which of course she hadn't. Either that, or some other person had been down to the woods the day Adele had gone missing. Some other person who shared this house with her.

Maybe it was time to start asking a few questions of the Feaver family. Perhaps one of them knew a great deal more than they were letting on about Adele's disappearance.

* * *

Six hours had passed. Six hours, during which time the suspended hush in the house Kim had grown used to gave way to a frenzy of activity. The tread of boots sent tremors around the house as members of the investigation team moved from room to room, opening drawers and cupboards while the occasional squawk of their walky-talkies blistered the air.

In the kitchen Kim washed up mugs and made tea, then washed up mugs again, all the time wondering about Adam Feaver sitting in an interview room down at the police station. Who'd be doing the interviewing? she wondered. Alan? Janice? Not herself, that was for sure.

Was she jealous? Maybe she'd have liked to be a fly on the wall, listening in to everything he said or trying to work out the implications of what he *didn't* say. But jealous, no. All this activity was down to her.

Returning to the house from the garden still clutching the battered bunch of foxgloves she'd retrieved from the bin, Kim had immediately cornered Sandra in the kitchen and ordered her to stop cleaning right away. Sandra had been resentful and thrilled in equal measure. Today was her morning for the Feavers, she complained. Friday was *always* her morning. There was no way she could come back tomorrow because she'd promised to look after her granddaughter while her daughter went off for a weekend mini-break with her son-in-law to try and patch up their marriage. There was the small matter of lost wages too.

But then her curiosity had taken over. *Why* did she have to stop cleaning? And what was all that about with the flowers? Was there something suspicious about them? Kim, refusing to be drawn, simply replied that she was sure there was no need to worry about losing pay and that it wouldn't matter if, for just this one week, the cleaning was left undone.

Then she'd hustled Sandra out of the back door and stood over her while she unlocked her bike to prevent her from entertaining any thoughts of hanging around the premises. Once back inside she'd immediately rung the investigation team, whereupon she'd been put through to the Super. *We'll follow it through. Thanks, Kim,* was all her boss had said once she'd heard Kim wonder if maybe Mrs Feaver had disappeared not from the wood but from the house.

When the call ended, Kim convinced herself the Super thought she was an idiot and that she should stop trying to pretend she was CID and stick to her role. But true to her word, the investigation team *did* follow it through. The Super called her back within half an hour to say that officers were en route to the house to pick up the flowers. They'd managed to get hold of one of the two forensic botanists in the county, who was already on her way over to compare the foxgloves in the house with the variety growing all over Linton Wood.

'Of course it's possible that Mrs Feaver picked these flowers earlier in the week,' she said. 'But given her movements for the days running up to her disappearance, I imagine she was far too preoccupied at college setting up this art display to go skipping off to the woods. Unless she picked them by moonlight, which is a bit unlikely.' Kim gave a grunt of agreement. 'Have you spoken to the kids?'

Kim was able to say that she had. 'Neither of them even remember seeing any flowers,' she said.

'That's kids for you,' the Super said, as if she'd had plenty of experience of the species.

'And Adam Feaver maintains he knows nothing about them either. He just assumes Adele had picked them from the garden.'

'He's not off the hook though. Husbands are always first to come under suspicion when a wife goes missing.'

'I guess.'

'We're going to have to interview him. Down at the nick this time, I think. Show we're serious. But the first thing we need to do is take DNA swabs and fingerprints. Including the cleaning lady.'

'Right.'

'She may not actually have left the house at all, you know,' the Super went on. 'She could still be there.' The silence that followed was ominous and pro- longed. 'There'll be a thorough search this time,' she added quietly.

'Still no sighting then?' Kim asked.

'None. No money's been taken from an ATM using her card anywhere either. It's not looking good.'

Kim wanted to say something. All the same, she hesitated. But what if it turned out to be important and she'd kept it to herself? Casting caution to the wind, she went ahead and described the scene in

Adam Feaver's study, where he'd made a few veiled comments about his wife's controlling nature. 'Maybe I should have mentioned it earlier,' she said. 'But I thought you might think I was reading too much into it.'

'Not at all,' the Super said. 'That's exactly the kind of insight you can give us as a FLO, being in such close proximity to the family.'

'There's something else I should mention too,' Kim said, encouraged by the Super's response. 'It's Emerson. He makes me uneasy.'

'In what way?'

'Something about his appearance for a start. The physique. The tattoos. The piercings. It's like this family is not his tribe. He doesn't say much, but what he does say sounds like he was born in 'da hood' and not in a leafy English village to a prosperous, artistic, educated family.'

'So are you accusing him of murdering his mother just because of the way he looks and sounds?' The Super's tone was sharp.

Kim was suddenly assailed by self-doubt. Was it just prejudice on her part? If so, then she deserved to be upbraided.

'It's not just the way he looks though,' she said, desperate to cover her tracks. 'It's his whole attitude. He seems indifferent to his mother's absence. As if it had no more significance to him than if the family cat had gone missing.'

There was a long pause in which the Super seemed to be considering Kim's words. 'Keep an eye on him,' she'd said at last. 'Keep an eye on all of them. Talk to them. Try and connect.' And then she said this: 'You're doing okay. Kim. All you need to do is keep watching and listening.'

* * *

Eloise was coming downstairs carrying a blue plastic basket full of dirty washing before her with both hands.

'Let me take that for you,' Kim said. 'It looks heavy.'

'If you want,' replied Eloise begrudgingly. But all the same, she allowed Kim to take it. 'Actually, now I can go back up and get the towels I couldn't carry,' she added, her manner almost civil this time.

'Good,' said Kim brightly. 'I'll see you down in the kitchen then.' Eloise, her thin shoulders slumped, plodded back upstairs wearily, like a woman four times her age.

'You seem to have got lumbered with all the domestic stuff,' Kim said when a couple of minutes later Eloise joined her, this time carrying a pile of dirty towels.

'Sandra would have put a load in but you sent her home.'

'I know. I'm sorry.'

'Doesn't matter. It's not your fault. I'm just worried about Dad. Why have they taken him to the police station? It's bad enough them asking for fingerprints and DNA. They can't possibly think any of us could have harmed Mum in any way.'

'It's just routine, Eloise. Like the DNA testing. Obviously your DNA is going to be all over this house. Your fingerprints too. We need to have a record of them so we can eliminate them. It's other people's DNA and fingerprints we're interested in.'

'Do you really think that Mum invited someone in, put flowers in a vase and then went off with them?'

'We don't know anything for certain,' Kim said. 'Right now, everything is just speculation.'

Eloise nodded. For a moment or two she simply stood there staring down at the pile of laundry, thinking her own thoughts. 'I don't know which I think is worse,' she said finally. 'If she was taken from the woods — kidnapped — that would have to be a stranger. But if she invited someone into the house, then that could only be a friend.'

'Yes,' Kim said in a small voice.

Eloise shuddered. 'But who? Who do we know that would do that? And where was Dad? Why didn't he come into the kitchen when he heard voices and stop it before it happened?' She gazed imploringly at Kim. 'I know what you're thinking,' she said. 'But it's not Dad.'

Kim didn't know what to say.

'It can't be him. If they've taken him to the police station because they think he killed her, then they're wrong.' There was an unsettling edge to her voice now.

'It's just routine, Eloise, like I said before,' Kim said in a bid to placate her. 'You mustn't upset yourself. They'll want to know if your dad heard or saw anything on the Sunday, that's all.'

Eloise nodded, calm once more. She glanced down at the laundry basket as if she'd suddenly remembered what she was doing here in the kitchen, standing by the washing machine. Finally she spoke. 'Emerson wears a T-shirt for half a day; then when one of his friends rings up to see if he wants to go out he chucks it in the wash and gets another from his drawer,' she said.

'I've never had a brother,' Kim said. 'But I have a younger sister. She was just the same. Thought there was a laundry fairy.' It was a nice surprise to see Eloise smile at her little joke. Finally, an opportunity to connect, just as the Super had urged. 'Course, she's changed now she has to do the family washing herself,' she added.

She stood back, allowing Eloise to take charge of both the washing and the conversation. Her judgement wasn't misplaced.

'Emerson's older than me, by five and a half years. But since his accident, Mum and Dad have treated him like the baby of the family.'

'Emerson had an accident?' Kim said.

'You must have noticed the limp, not to mention the other stuff.' She poured far too much washing liquid into the little plastic ball and flung it into the machine after the towels. 'The slightly vacant look, like he's just woken up or he isn't listening, or both. The temper tantrums when things don't go his way.' Some excess washing liquid had dribbled down the front of the drum and slid onto the floor, but Eloise didn't bother to wipe it up. Instead she pushed the drum door firmly shut and got up from her knees. 'Though so far you've been lucky not to have witnessed one of those.'

'What happened?' Kim wanted to know.

'It was about five years ago. He was a passenger in his friend's car. The friend was driving like a maniac. Wrapped the

136

car round a tree. A pedestrian was killed.'

'No! How awful! Did the friend survive?'

'Oh yes. He was prosecuted for dangerous driving. Sent to prison for six months, and lost his licence. Emerson was in a coma for about six weeks. Nobody thought he'd recover.'

'He looks fit enough now,' Kim said.

'He worked at it. Still does. He's obsessive. Drags himself to the gym every day for a workout,' she said.

'Yes, I can see. The results are pretty impressive,' Kim said.

Eloise pulled a face. '*Some* girls seem to like the look,' she said. 'Sub-Ryan Gosling, I call it. He's got the pecs and the limp and the tattoos. But he isn't Ryan Gosling.'

'No. But Ryan Gosling's a hard act to follow, wouldn't you say?'

Eloise smiled again, showing off her exquisite cheekbones.

'It must have been awful for you all,' Kim said.

She shrugged. 'Worse for Mum and Dad and Emerson, of course. I was thirteen at the time. I remember I used to sulk because Mum and Dad fussed over Emerson so much. I was convinced they'd forgotten they had a daughter. Kids, eh?' She rolled her eyes in self-disparagement.

'Understandable, I guess. What happened to the friend?'

'Oh, we don't see him anymore. The two of them used to be inseparable. But after the accident Aaron became persona non grata. Everyone turned against him. Not just Mum and Dad but school friends too,' she said. 'I guess they thought that Emerson was never going to come out of the coma, or he might end up brain damaged or paraplegic. Aaron tried to make amends. He came round one night when I was up in bed, and there was an almighty row. Dad sent him packing. And that was that.'

Eloise shrugged her shoulders matter-of-factly. Case closed, she seemed to say. The sound of tyres on gravel and the slamming of a car door put an end to the conversation. 'Dad's back,' Eloise said. 'See, what did I say?'

Kim felt slightly uneasy at the thought of meeting Adam again. Would his previously friendly manner towards her have changed? Those odd things he'd said about Adele could only have got back to the police through her, and he'd have realised that immediately.

She would have slipped away and left father and daughter alone together. But Adam was already there, strolling nonchalantly through the kitchen door before Kim could make her escape.

'Oh, good. Somebody's tackling the laundry at last. I'm dangerously close to my last pair of pants.' He went to kiss his daughter while at the same time acknowledging Kim with his usual friendly smile.

Eloise wrinkled her nose fastidiously. 'Dad!' she said. 'Not sure either of us needs to know that.'

'How about a decent cup of coffee to take away the taste of that nasty stuff they gave me down the police station? Care to join us, Kim?'

He hadn't used her first name before. She relaxed. Of course the investigation team wouldn't have quoted what he'd

139

told her in a private conversation. They needed him to co-operate, and Kim was the means whereby that co-operation could be achieved and upheld.

'I'll pass if you don't mind,' she said. 'I need to get on with a couple of things.'

He made a rueful face. 'Just you and me then, Elly,' he said. 'Come and sit down and I'll tell you all about it. Must say, it's been a fascinating experience. Given me a brilliant idea for a new novel!'

★　★　★

Janice rang just as Kim was getting into her car to drive home at the end of the day. She put her phone on hands-free, turned on the engine and drove away.

'We've got nothing on him,' she'd said, when Kim asked how the interview had *really* gone. 'He was still sticking to his story that he'd been locked in his study all weekend and hadn't gone to bed. As for those flowers, he's simply assuming they came from the garden, which is where he'd glimpsed Adele some time Sunday, he can't remember when.

Anyway, that's why I'm ringing you,' Janice went on. 'To tell you that the flowers are — to quote the report — incontrovertibly from Linton Wood.'

'What does it mean, Janice?' Kim said.

'Haven't a Scooby, Kim. In fact we're all at a total loss. That's the other reason I'm calling. The Super wants a televised press appeal tomorrow at six thirty. You need to prepare them, 'cause they'll have seen them on the telly and they'll know it usually means the worst.'

Tomorrow was going to be hard. If only Kim could go home and put her feet up. But there was dinner to make first. She'd asked Dad to change the beds before she'd left but she didn't suppose he'd bothered, so she was going to have to do that too.

'What about your day? Pick up anything useful?'

Janice's question reminded her that compared to what was going on in the Feaver household at the moment, she didn't have much to complain about. She filled Janice in quickly. The boys had left pretty well empty-handed as far as she could tell. 'You know what they're like. Everything has to be top-secret with them,' she said. 'But some good news. I think I've finally got through to Eloise. We had a real chat this afternoon.' She told Janice the details of their conversation.

'I said you'd win them over in the end,' Janice said.

'I'm not getting anywhere with Emerson. But now I know about his accident and how much it set him back, I'm wondering if that explains his slightly off-kilter behaviour.'

She'd reached home. 'I'd better go now, Janice,' she said reluctantly. 'Duty calls.'

'Don't you mean off-duty?'

'If only I did,' she said as, with a sigh, she ended the call.

Kim's spirits were low as she let herself inside the house. But then she caught a whiff of something good coming from the cooker. 'Dad?' she said as she followed her nose into the kitchen.

The table was set for dinner, though there was no sign of Dad. Hearing him moving around overhead, she climbed the stairs.

'Oh. You gave me a shock,' he said, coming out of his bedroom door. 'I've just been changing the beds.'

This was getting better and better. 'Are you all right, Dad?' she said.

'Never better,' he said. 'How about you?'

There was something he wasn't saying. She followed him downstairs and into the kitchen. Sooner or later she'd get to the bottom of it. 'What's cooking?' she asked, sniffing the air theatrically.

'Lasagne,' he said. 'And there's salad to go with it. All you need to do is sit down and eat it.'

She watched him remove the lasagne from the cooker and plate it up — rather inelegantly, but she had no intention of complaining. 'It looks lovely, Dad,' she said, pulling out her chair and sitting down.

It tasted even lovelier. They ate in silence until they'd finished. Then Dad put down his knife and fork, cleared his throat and took a sip of water. It was clear that he was about to make an announcement.

'I just want to say that I'm sorry for being so selfish since your mum . . . '

Kim let her knife and fork drop on her plate. What on earth had brought this on?

'I've had your sister round this afternoon. She brought the lasagne, as you've probably guessed.'

'Well, it had sort of occurred to me.' But, Shannon bringing round food? What had got into her?

'She told me about that case you're working on, and how stressful it must be for you. She said I wasn't pulling my weight and she was here to tell me so because you never would.'

Kim opened her mouth to regurgitate the usual words of reassurance she had off pat these days. But he put up his hand to shush her. Shannon was right, he said. He'd been too wrapped up in his own grief to see that Kim was grieving too. And then he'd expected her to take on all the chores on top of doing her job.

'Well, from today it's all change,' he said. 'Shannon brought me this.' He was still wearing Mum's old apron and from one of its deep pockets he withdrew a piece of paper. 'She printed it off,' he said. 'There's a course for men like me — widowers — who've never learned to cook. She's made me promise to join up.'

That was the difference between Shannon and herself, in a nutshell. Whereas Kim liked to think she cajoled, Shannon threatened. It seemed Shannon's way was the most effective.

She could hear her phone ringing from the hallway.

'You'd better get that,' he said. 'It's probably important. I'll clear the dishes and get the pudding.'

'Right.' Cooking classes? Clear the dishes? Pudding?

She got to the phone just before it went to voicemail. It was Janice.

'The name of that guy,' she said urgently, 'the one who caused Emerson Feaver's accident. What was it?'

Kim racked her brains. 'Aaron something,' she said.

'Aaron Rothwell.' She wasn't asking, she was confirming.

'Might be. She didn't say. Why?'

'Because we've got a DNA match and a partial fingerprint for him.'

Kim was puzzled. 'But that can't be,' she said. 'I told you what Eloise said. Since he caused Emerson's accident five years ago he's been persona non grata at their house.'

'All the more reason we need to find him, Kim,' Janice said. 'And urgently.'

★ ★ ★

Kim had gathered the family together in the front room in order to deliver the news. Neither Eloise nor Emerson looked particularly happy at being dragged out of bed at ten in the morning — it was clearly the crack of dawn for them.

'Aaron Rothwell in our kitchen? How?' Eloise, tugging at the belt of her pink towelling bathrobe, furrowed her brow. Even with her bed-head hair and a face devoid of make-up, she was still a stunning beauty.

Emerson, slumped on the settee, yawned and scratched his head. His bathrobe was navy. Two rather large white feet attached to a pair of skinny, hairy white legs protruded from beneath it. The work-out, apparently, was restricted to his upper body only. Had the information computed yet? Kim wondered.

'Did you know about this, Dad?' Eloise was tense with nerves. She glanced over at Adam, slouching against the doorframe and fumbling for a cigarette. Kim had noticed the past couple of days that smoking no longer seemed out of bounds anywhere in the house.

He shook his head but said nothing. Kim sensed he was taking refuge behind his cigarette.

'We're looking for him,' Kim said. 'You must all be assured of that.'

'Are you saying he's kidnapped Mum?' Eloise said.

Emerson snorted. 'Kidnapped,' he repeated, a flicker of amusement crossing his face. 'Aaron's a nutter!'

'We can't be sure,' Kim said, furrowing her brow at Emerson's tasteless remark. 'We've been in touch with his mother, but she says he hasn't lived at home permanently for at least four years. She gave us an address in London but it was a shared house. The people living there now have no idea where he went after he moved out. He didn't leave a forwarding address.'

'So what now?' Adam spoke at last, his question accompanied by a thin exhalation of smoke. All Kim could do was repeat what she'd been told: that the Superintendent in charge of the case was anxious for the family to step in front of the cameras and do an appeal this evening.

'TV? No way!' Eloise shook her head vehemently.

Kim stumbled on, hoping to change her mind. It would have been a good idea even without this new turn of events, she said. But now it was even more important to get Adele's face out there and to try to jog the public's memory. 'She may be in danger, remember,' she ended by saying.

'All right,' Eloise said when Kim had finished speaking. 'But don't ask me to say anything. Dad can do the talking.'

Kim glanced at Adam. He looked

148

uncomfortable, she thought.

'Will they give me a script?' he said, his voice hoarse.

Didn't he appear at literary festivals, speaking to rows of fans about his books? Show up at libraries and talk to book clubs? 'If you need a script then we'll write one for you,' she said. 'But it would sound much better if what you said came from the heart.'

'Yes,' he said. 'I'm sure that's true. It's just . . . ' He trailed off, leaving Kim wondering, *It's just what, exactly?* That he was rubbish with words? Well, that couldn't be true, could it?

'We'll talk about the logistics later, shall we?' she said.

'Well if you're done I'm going back to bed.' Emerson dragged himself off the settee and made for the door.

From her seat next to his, Eloise shot him a look of disdain. 'I'm going for a run,' she pronounced, pulling herself up. 'I can't bear all this sitting around.'

'What about you, Adam?' Kim asked when she'd gone.

Adam strolled over to the window and

stared vacantly at the view. He had stuff to do, he mumbled.

'Anything I can help you with?' She didn't think he looked too great. Not ill, exactly, but preoccupied. This information about Aaron Rothwell — and the possible implications of it — must have been very distressing for him.

He should check the messages on the house phone, he said, but he really couldn't be bothered with people incessantly asking him how he was and if there was any news.

'I'll do it,' she said. 'Why don't you grab some coffee? Maybe try and get some rest?'

'Yes,' he said listlessly. 'I'll take it upstairs.'

It was the work of a good twenty minutes to take the messages. There were a couple from Adam's agent, concerned that Adam wasn't answering his mobile. Most of the others, however, were from concerned well-wishers in the village, just as Adam had feared. After the appeal tonight there'd be many more of these, Kim mused as she put

150

down the phone at last.

She was just about to walk away when it started ringing. She recognised the voice on the other end immediately. It was Michael.

'What are you doing there?' He sounded flustered when she greeted him like an old friend.

Briefly she explained her role. 'Didn't your assistant tell you I'd popped in the other day with Adam's apologies?' she asked.

'Well, she said a police officer had been,' he said. 'If she'd said it was you I'd have rung sooner.'

Now it was her turn to be flustered. Anyway, what could she do for him? she asked once she'd composed herself. Did he want to speak to Adam? Only, now might not be a good time.

'No, no. I don't want to bother him,' Michael said. 'Perhaps you can pass on my best wishes and tell him not to worry about cancelling his talk. Hopefully he'll be in a position to do it another time.' He paused, then added, 'Oh, dear. That sounds rather callous, doesn't it? But what *does* one say in cases like this?'

'It's difficult,' she agreed.

Another pause, then he said: 'I — er — while you're on the phone, Kim, I wondered . . . '

'Yes?'

'I know you're keen on Seraphine Masters, the historical crime writer.'

Fancy him remembering that. They'd had a chat about her Lord St John Stokes series and discovered they were both huge fans.

'It's just . . . I managed to nab her to do a talk later in the month. I wonder if you might be able to get someone to sit with your father and come along to it.'

'Oh!' Her insides did a little dance as she considered his invitation.

'Of course, I'll quite understand if you feel you can't leave him.'

'I'd love to come,' she said before he could talk her out of turning him down. 'My dad seems much improved recently.'

'Splendid! Then it's a date,' he said.

It certainly looked like it might be, she thought as she replaced the receiver in a daze. A cup of coffee might be just the thing to calm her down. She followed the aroma into the kitchen. Adam was sitting at the table, staring into space, yet another cigarette hanging from his fingers. He looked even worse than he'd done earlier.

'Adam? Are you OK?'

'Actually no,' he said, a hopeless expression in his faraway gaze.

'What is it?'

But before he could reply, there was an almighty clatter of feet running down the stairs. Eloise flew into the kitchen, her long hair streaming out behind her, dishevelled in her bathrobe and holding out her phone.

'It's Mum,' she said. 'She's sent me a message. She wants me to go and meet her.'

'Let me see.' Kim reached out to take the phone, her heart beating fast.

The message was a simple one: *Can't come home just now. But long to meet. Need to explain.* Then she'd typed an address. It was a house in a street in Brandsford. Kim recognised the name — Rothwell Street. The houses there were

153

Victorian — three-storey affairs, mostly flats.

'You can't go, Eloise,' Kim said. 'Not until I've checked it out with the Super.'

'What do you mean?'

'It could be a trap,' Kim said. 'Just because this message is coming from your mum's phone, it doesn't necessarily mean she sent it.'

'It's not a trap.' Adam's words, muttered from behind his hands, were muffled. Kim and Eloise stared at him intently, both waiting for him to explain himself.

'Adele's with *him*,' he said at last. 'Aaron Rothwell. They arrived here together last Sunday and they left together less than half an hour later. We didn't argue. She said that though Aaron could forgive Emerson and me, she didn't think she could. And then she left. After she'd gone I arranged the flowers in the vase and thought what a mess I'd made of everything.'

Both Kim and Eloise gaped at him, open-mouthed.

'Is this true?' Kim said.

Adam nodded.

'They're having an affair?' Eloise said. 'She's left you to go and live with a boy young enough to be her son?'

Adam shook his head. 'No, it's not like that,' he said. 'He'd offered to put her up for a while, that was all, she said.'

'And you believed her?' Eloise demanded. It was clear that *she* didn't.

Kim's brain started to race. This was a case of wasting police time. How and why had Adam Feaver let things drag on so long? Then there was this damn public appeal tonight. *That* would have to be cancelled. But first, she needed to get to the bottom of Adam's convoluted story.

'Yes, I do believe her,' Adam said. 'Adele doesn't tell lies. *She's* not the liar in the house.'

'What exactly does Aaron need to forgive you for?' Kim asked. And what on earth did he mean by his cryptic remark?

Adam gave her a pleading look. She must believe him, he said. He'd only done what he'd done because he loved his family and wanted to protect them.

'Please, Dad,' Eloise said, 'you're not

making any sense.'

Perhaps they should allow the clearly troubled Adam to explain, Kim said.

'But where do I start?' he asked. 'It's a long story.'

'Then start at the beginning,' Kim replied. 'I'll put the kettle on.'

She had a feeling they were going to be here for a long time.

★ ★ ★

'They were best friends once, Emerson and Aaron. They met at secondary school and hung out together right through till sixth form, when Emerson's accident happened,' Adam began.

They'd finished for the summer — all that was left was for them to do their exams. 'A' students, both of them, he added, though each talented in different ways.

'Emerson had accepted an offer to do life sciences at Manchester University. Aaron was all set to do an arts foundation course. He was Adele's top student. And he was besotted with her.'

Eloise shuddered. 'Don't,' she said. 'You're creeping me out.'

'If he hadn't had those feelings for her then, he wouldn't have done what he did,' he went on. 'But I'm getting ahead of myself.'

He took another cigarette from the packet and held it between his fingers, playing with it as he spoke. What he wanted to do was tell her about the night of the accident, he said.

'We bought him — Emerson — a car for his eighteenth birthday. Adele was against it. I should have listened to her. That very night he took Aaron for a spin and ended up in a coma.'

'*Emerson* took Aaron for a spin?' Eloise said, aghast. 'But it was Aaron at the wheel. He hit a pedestrian and killed them. Ended up in jail for it.'

'What happened?' an equally stunned Kim asked him.

'I'll tell you exactly what happened, Kim,' Adam said, turning towards her. 'It was Emerson at the wheel when he was hugely over the limit. It was Emerson who drove into that pedestrian and killed

157

him, then just drove on. And when the car came to a standstill wrapped round a tree, it was Aaron, with no alcohol or drugs in his system, who pulled his best friend out of the driver's seat and somehow managed to get him into the passenger seat.'

'No!' Eloise began to sob loudly but Adam ignored her and continued to speak.

'When the police and the ambulance turned up they discovered Emerson unconscious and Aaron, next to him, at the wheel,' he said.

A sudden shadow crossed the room. When Kim looked up she saw Emerson in the doorway, fully clothed at last.

'Dad, what the hell are you doing?' His face was contorted in fury and he was shaking. 'You promised me you'd keep what happened secret. This is a police officer you're talking to! Do you want to see me in prison?'

Kim had been with the family almost a week now. In all that time this was the longest speech she'd ever heard Emerson make.

'You were happy enough to see Aaron go down for something he didn't do,' Adam snarled back at his son. 'Your best friend. Now your mother's discovered how we both let him go ahead and take the rap for it. And she's disowned us for it.'

'How?' Emerson wanted to know. 'How did she find out?'

'Because Aaron told her. Last month. She bumped into him at some gallery or other in London. He had a job there, helping the owner out, she said. *A great waste of his talents* was how she described it to me later.'

Emerson turned his head away. It was as if he thought by doing that he could avoid hearing everything his father went on to explain. Eloise had sunk into a chair. She gripped the table top with both hands, her fingertips white.

'He told her and she came home and confronted me. I couldn't deny it. She said I had to go to the police with the truth. I said I couldn't. That not only would Emerson get into trouble, but us too, for perverting the cause of justice.'

Finally Adam put the cigarette he'd been playing with so long between his lips and lit it. 'I hoped she'd seen reason, because she didn't bring the subject up again. But of course, looking back, I knew I was fooling myself. I'd already lost her. She was just biding her time. The afternoon she came back with Aaron, she told me she'd rung him from the woods where she'd been walking and picking flowers to calm herself down.' He tipped the lengthening ash off his cigarette. 'She'd told him she couldn't stay with me anymore, but she couldn't turn her own son in either. She was distraught. He met her on the edge of the woods and drove her back here. She wanted to tell me to my face that she was leaving, she said. Because unlike me, she wasn't a coward.'

'But why did Aaron say he'd killed someone when he hadn't?' Eloise said.

'Because he knew how precious Emerson was to your mother. Remember, we all thought Emerson was going to die. What a legacy for a mother to have — a drunken, coked-up son who'd killed someone.'

Eloise turned on her brother. 'And you let him do this for you?' she yelled. 'Ruin his reputation and all his future chances?'

'I was in a coma, in case you've forgotten. By the time I came out of it he'd already been sentenced.'

'But you could have stopped it! Had the decision reversed.'

Emerson shrugged.

'You creep,' Eloise said. 'And you, Dad. How could you?'

'I'm sorry. I deserve your contempt just as much as I deserve your mother's. It was terrible what I did. When Aaron came round to the house and told me what had really happened just after he'd been arrested, I sent him packing. Told him to keep right away from me, my wife and my children. Told him I didn't believe him and that Adele wouldn't believe him either.'

Death by dangerous driving; perverting the cause of justice; wasting police time. It was hard to keep up with the list of crimes these two had notched up between the two of them.

'I told Adele he'd been round to the

house telling me a pack of lies,' he went on. 'She believed me, of course. But if she'd seen his face she'd have known, just like I did, that he was telling the truth. When Emerson came home from hospital, after Aaron had been convicted and sent down, I asked him if there was any truth in Aaron's story. And he admitted what really happened.'

'It was your idea to forget everything, remember?' Emerson said accusingly, levelling his father with an angry stare. 'You said Aaron would be out in months and then he'd be able to get on with his life. So we should just get on with ours.'

'You two are unbelievable,' Eloise hissed. 'It's not surprising Mum decided to bail out of this family. I intend to do the same thing myself.' She got up from her seat. Turning to Kim, she announced that she was going to phone her mother immediately and make arrangements to go and see her. 'And don't try to stop me,' she ended by saying.

Kim had no intentions of doing any such thing. She had something much more urgent to do. She got to her feet.

Solemnly and determinedly, she made the arrests and read each of them their rights.

* * *

A month had passed. It was high time she got it over with, Shannon had said, and introduced poor Michael to Dad. When Kim suggested inviting him for dinner, Dad insisted on doing the cooking.

Would he have time with all his other commitments? Kim wanted to know. It wasn't just cookery classes these days. He'd also joined the ramblers and taken up bowls, thanks to the new friends he'd made. Then there were his regular swimming and tai chi sessions.

Leave it with me, he'd said. *It's only a bit of dinner.*

A bit of dinner, however, was exactly what it wasn't. The starter of asparagus with Serrano ham and a chive-and-walnut dressing had been delicious. However, it had been accompanied by a long tale of the lengths he'd gone to get the correct type of asparagus — only the superior white would do. No one else had been able to get a word in edgewise.

Now they were on to the mains while desert, a tarte tatin, languished on top of the cooker cooling, and Dad was showing no signs of flagging. If ever she got stuck for a dessert in the future, Kim believed that after Dad's lecture on how to cook a perfect tarte tatin, she'd be able to pull it off. Same with this recipe for salmon with a herb-and-Parmesan crust too, probably.

'Simplest thing in the world,' he said, handing round the crushed potatoes with a flourish. 'Blitz your breadcrumbs with some Parmesan and a handful of parsley. Add lime juice and some olive oil to bind everything together, and press it down on your salmon steaks.'

Michael made his *how interesting* face. He'd been making it all through Dad's analysis of the best apple to use in a tarte tatin, and throughout his one-man debate — crème fraiche or double cream — and it looked like it might have stuck.

'The secret is a hot oven. That way you get the crispy crust,' he went on.

'Delicious, Dad,' Kim said.

Shannon would have shut him up ages

ago; said it outright — *D'you think we can just get on with it now?* But Kim was in a mellow mood. Another couple of weeks and she'd be back in a place of her own. It had been Dad's idea. She'd run around after him long enough and he was very grateful. But he was back on form now; and besides, now she had a boyfriend, didn't she deserve some privacy?

Boyfriend! Kim glanced up from her plate at Michael, with his grey hair that was thinning on top and the creases round his eyes she found so endearing. It had been a while since Michael had been a boy!

She wished there was a word to describe the relationship between two people who'd recently grown very close. Man-friend sounded a bit, well . . . seedy; and the word 'friend' on its own had an air of coyness about it to her ears. She'd just have to stick to using his name. If she said it often enough people would soon get the picture. Meanwhile, next time she got the urge to suggest a meal, perhaps they should head for a restaurant.

The Lowri Letters

Lowri sat at the kitchen table on the least rickety chair, surrounded by the detritus of breakfast. What was it about teenagers that they were always in too much of a hurry to clear away their breakfast things, yet they were never short of time to Facebook friends they'd be seeing half an hour later?

She struggled to apply herself to the sums she'd scrawled on the back of an envelope — coincidentally, the one that had initially contained a red electricity bill — until she tucked it away in one of the kitchen drawers with the other unpaid bills.

How could she make this set of figures add up? She shifted position so that she didn't have to look at the cooker. One of the rings had given up the ghost and, because it was wildly out of guarantee, that meant she'd have to pay someone to come and fix it. Sadly, the manoeuvre only brought her face to face with the scuffed paintwork on the opposite wall.

Count your blessings, Lowri, she told herself sternly. *At least you have a roof over your head, even if that roof has several tiles missing. Be thankful you're not living on the street with all your worldly possessions bundled into two carrier bags.*

The phone rang. Perhaps it was one of those TV makeover programmes offering to do up her house for free. The very idea put a smile on her face. But when she heard her ex-husband's voice it quickly faded.

'Lowri — finally! Do you ever listen to your messages?'

Lowri swore silently. Whenever Patrick called it was never for anything she wanted to hear. 'What is it, Patrick? I'm just on my way out,' she lied.

'It's about the house.' There was a pause. 'Cressida and I both agree we need a bigger place.'

So it was getting serious with his latest, then. She almost felt sorry for the girl — she couldn't possibly know what she

170

was getting into. Monogamy had never come easily to Patrick, as Lowri had discovered early on in her marriage. She'd forgiven one but she'd drawn the line at two. They'd been separated for two years now, divorced for one. Cressida had arrived on the scene six months ago.

'And the only way we're going to be able to get one is if you sell up and give me my half of the value.'

She reminded him as calmly as she could that this was the familial home. She needed a house with three bedrooms. Besides, he'd agreed she could keep the house when they split up. It wasn't as if she'd asked for anything else, after all.

'Cressida and I want to start our own family. Until you move out and get somewhere smaller, we're stuck where we are.'

What? She gripped the receiver hard. He *had* a family! Felix and Megan. Why did he need to start another at his advanced age?

'Things change, Lowri. The twins are growing up. They'll be off to uni next year.'

Oh, this was preposterous! She reminded him of the average length of the academic year — although as a university lecturer he shouldn't need reminding. What were Felix and Megan meant to do for the other twenty-two weeks? she demanded.

'I don't know. Sleep on the sofa. Stay with friends.'

'You're unbelievable,' Lowri muttered.

'No, *you're* unbelievable! I just want what's mine, that's all. I've been reasonable long enough. Put the house on the market or buy me out.'

'And how the hell do you expect me to do that on a part-time primary teacher's salary?'

'I don't know. Sell something. What about those love letters you've still got from wotsisface? The famous rock star, your childhood sweetheart? Somebody would pay good money for those.'

Well, well, well. So that was it. This was no spur-of-the-moment idea. He'd obviously planned to bring up Elliot's letters before he made this call. Talked it over with Cressida too, no doubt.

What a team they made.

'I mean it, Lowri,' he said. 'This time next year there could be three of us. We need a home just as much as you and the kids do. You can't hang on to the house indefinitely.'

'I hear you,' she said flatly. 'Now if you don't mind, I've got stuff I need to get on with.'

And with that, she replaced the receiver.

* * *

The first time she'd met Patrick, she was twenty-three and she and Elliot had been over and done with for five years. Rubicon, Elliot's band, had broken the States and, as far as she knew, nowadays he was living the high life somewhere on the west coast. There were rumours in the press that his girlfriend was pregnant, and more rumours that despite this fact Elliot was seeing other girls.

Funny how she seemed destined to be drawn to men who were constitutionally unable to commit. But of course, back then, that first night she met Patrick, she wasn't to know that he and Elliot had faithlessness in common. Patrick was just a charming guest; an intriguing older man she'd met at a friend's dinner party.

'Put Rubicon on,' someone demanded when all the food had been eaten and enough wine had been drunk to make the conversation flow. '*The First Album.*'

In the silence between the needle being lowered and the initial haunting strains of the flute that introduced the first track, Lowri found herself making her announcement. 'Elliot Hogan and I were childhood sweethearts, you know,' she said.

The reaction was exactly how it always was. Mouths dropped open, eyes widened and everyone began talking at once, bombarding her with questions. When? Where did they meet? What was he like? What happened to break them up?

'Oh, you know, the usual. We drifted apart. He got signed and the band moved here to London in the summer just after we'd done our A-levels and were waiting for the results. I stayed in the Welsh village where we both grew up, working in the local pub to earn some money till it was time for college. We exchanged letters for a while, but communication just petered out once the band started to get big in the States. The rest, as they say, is history.'

It was a script she'd rehearsed many times; an accomplished performance she accompanied with a wry smile. *You win some, you lose some*, her self-deprecating shrug seemed to suggest. *And, hey, I'm over it.*

She believed it was from that moment that Patrick properly noticed her for the first time. For the rest of the evening he gave her his full attention. He loved her Welsh lilt, he told her. What was it like growing up on a farm? Did she miss the mountains? And was it true that all Welsh people could sing?

That night, seduced by the wine and the warmth and the background sound of Elliot's mournful singing, she began to truly believe that she was ready to move forward and embrace a new romance at last.

Elliot had been a boy when she knew him. The songs he'd written and played and that she'd once found so profound now sounded self-indulgent, shallow and trite. They were a pleasant backdrop, nothing more. The main performers this evening were herself and Patrick, growing ever more attracted to each other as the evening progressed.

When she moved in with him less than three months later and she suggested it was probably time to throw Elliot's letters away, Patrick wouldn't hear of it. Perhaps it was because he was an academic, he said. But burning those letters would be like wiping out history. And so, laughingly, she'd agreed to keep them.

After she put the phone down, Lowri went upstairs. The letters were where she'd kept them all these years, held together with a red rubber band in a shoebox on top of the wardrobe mixed up with other souvenirs of her past — teeny-tiny nametags both Felix and Megan had worn around their wrists as newborn babies; a treasured note to Father Christmas Felix had scribbled when he'd been six; baby teeth and locks of hair; the children's first bootees; their first school reports; and a few old school books of her own, some written in Welsh, which had been her first language.

She tugged at the elastic band, breaking it in her impatience, whereupon the letters fell higgledy-piggledy onto the bed. There were no more than a dozen, the handwriting faded on the yellowing envelopes. She picked up a letter at random. No address; just a date: September 1985.

My darling Lowri, it read, *life is a drag without you by my side*. There was a lot of that sort of thing in these early missals. Complaints about the hours spent in the recording studio and how awful it was having to share a flat with the other guys in the band — John, Gary, Pete, and the new guy Tony, who none of them had wanted and no one liked but who the manager had insisted would bring a different sound to the group. Occasionally he'd make a reference to their shared past at school, the walks they'd taken, the places they'd visited, Sunday afternoons spent in his bedroom when his parents had been visiting his gran in the next valley.

But as the letters progressed he stopped asking her when she could visit him. The melancholy tone changed to excited anticipation at the prospect of the release of their first album. He described parties he'd been to and people he'd met — no girls, oddly, which would have made someone a bit more worldly than herself suspicious. *Last night I got drunk with Mick Jagger*, one letter boasted. *What a geezer!*

There were more anecdotes like this — amusing, outrageous in many cases, all involving people who'd been in the public eye back in the day. *People would pay good money for those.* Patrick's words came back to her. How much money, exactly? Enough to enable her to buy Patrick out and keep the house?

She didn't want to move. She loved this house. The children had been born here. It was their home. Why should she move to some pokey hovel just so that Patrick could buy somewhere grander for him and Cressida and her biological clock?

Moving out, moving on
The past before us, our future gone
Baby kisses, baby shoes,
Tender treasures, marriage blues.

Funny how it happened that words popped into her head whenever she found herself deep in thought. Little stories that always rhymed. Songs without music. Ever since she'd been a teenager. But now wasn't the time to be inventing rhymes. She was a grown-up now with grown-up problems.

How did you go about finding a buyer for something you wanted to sell that might eventually bring you the kind of money you needed to stop you worrying about your finances for a while? What was it she always said to the kids when they asked her questions to do with their coursework that she had no answer for? *Google it*, that was it.

'No time like the present,' she said to the empty room, slipping a hair bobble she'd found next to the bed around her precious cargo before returning it to its shoebox.

Mr Partridge, of Partridge and Paige, *valuers and auctioneers for over one hundred years*, according to the firm's website, was round and bald and enthusiastic. On meeting her he shook her hand profusely before offering her a seat and cheerily demanding to know how he could be of assistance.

'Fascinating,' he said after she'd stammered out her story. 'I must admit to being rather partial to a bit of Rubicon myself.'

There was something about this remark, delivered as it was by a man whose conventional appearance gave the impression that his tastes were more likely to run along easy listening lines rather than prog rock, that made Lowri want to giggle.

'You'll want to see them then,' she said, struggling to keep a straight face as she handed over the bundle. 'To check they're genuine, I mean.'

As she watched this stranger turn the pages of her private correspondence, her buoyant mood left her and she began to feel ill at ease. She felt the same kind of discomfort she suspected she'd feel if she discovered someone rummaging through her underwear drawer. She was on the point of saying that she'd changed her mind and didn't want to sell after all when he suddenly stopped reading, looked up and spoke.

Alas, it was as he'd suspected. Fascinating as the letters appeared to be even on a quick skimming, he didn't think that Partridge and Paige were quite the people she was looking for, he said. She was almost relieved.

But then he added that there *was* someone he could recommend — an Alan Lincoln, who dealt exclusively in anything to do with pop culture. He didn't have a number for him to hand, but if Lowri were to leave it with him . . .

He seemed so eager to help, and so encouraging about the chances of her making a real killing if she went with this other character, that Lowri found herself meekly handing over her number. She reminded herself that

181

however uncomfortable it made her, selling the letters was all in a good cause — to keep a roof over her head and those of her children, and to get Patrick off her back once and for all.

Getting on with her life once she'd shaken the dust of Partridge and Paige off her feet proved easier than she'd imagined. She was just too busy to spare a thought for Alan Lincoln and when and if he'd get back to her.

The reception class teacher was off sick, so Lowri jumped in right away, volunteering to cover on her days off. The extra money meant she could call out the electrician to fix her wonky cooker, which was a cause of huge celebration in the house when she announced it.

Teaching reception was an exhausting affair. There was no rest at home, either. Evenings were spent doing the chores and planning lessons. By Friday evening she was exhausted. She was opening a bottle of wine in the kitchen, offering up a silent prayer of thanks that she'd made it through the week, when the phone rang.

'Get that, will you, Megan?' she called

out. 'If it's your dad, I'm in the bath.' The last thing she wanted was another conversation about putting the house on the market.

'It's for you, Mum,' Megan called out from the hall. 'Some man.'

Lowri caught her breath. It must be Alan Lincoln. What had he decided? Would he take the letters and put them up for auction? Or was he ringing to say that she'd be lucky to get twenty quid for them? She filled her glass, took a long slug, topped it up, then took it through to the hall.

'Hello,' she said.

There was a long pause. Finally someone spoke. 'Lowri. It's me. I'm glad I caught you in.'

She would have recognised that Welsh lilt anywhere, even overlaid with the odd American vowel. 'Elliot?'

'Alan Lincoln gave me your number. He thought I should know that you were planning to sell my letters.'

She struggled to take in what he was saying. Was this really Elliot, ringing her after all these years so casually? The man who'd broken her young heart?

'Well, you've got a nerve after all this time,' she said, half-joking, half-serious.

There was a beat, followed by a nervous laugh, as if Elliot wasn't sure quite how to take what she'd said.

'You're right. You deserve an explanation,' Elliot said. 'I was a bastard, pure and simple. I got too full of myself. Started to believe the hype. I was a young man with the world at my feet. You know how it is.'

Lowri was suddenly twenty again. How vulnerable she'd been. His apology sounded more like a proud boast. *Look at me, I'm Jack the Lad — but, hey, everyone loves a bad boy.*

'So, what are you doing now?' she asked him.

He spoke at length, the gist being that he'd had enough of the LA scene. The weather, the people, the limelight. And he was so tired of dodging the paparazzi.

'Which brings me back to the letters,' he said.

Oh, yes, the letters.

'Lowri. You can't sell them.'

'Can't I? Why not?'

'I'm back in the UK now. Been back in Wales about three months. I own a small farm, in fact. And I'm a private citizen these days. I've been in the public eye for too long and I don't want it anymore. All I want is to farm my sheep, collect my art and my wine, and live a normal life.'

Poor you, she almost said. How awful it must be to be rich and famous. Farming sheep, collecting art, wine-drinking. Was this what a normal life consisted of in Elliot's world? How similar this forty-odd-year-old Elliot sounded to the twenty-year-old one, with his complaints about sharing a flat with his fellow bandmates in that letter she'd re-read only last week. And had he asked her anything about herself? No. Not one single question. Selfish and self-obsessed, just like he'd always been.

'Those letters are mine to do anything I want with,' she said.

There was a pause, and then he answered, 'I'm not sure a lawyer would see it that way, Lowri.'

A trickle of fear ran through her. Could

he do that — bring fancy lawyers in to stop her getting the money she needed to keep her family home? But hot on the heels of her fear was fury. Those letters were addressed to her; therefore she owned them.

'You've changed, Elliot,' she said bitterly. 'But you can't frighten me.' Before he could say another word, she slammed down the phone. Then she knocked back her wine and marched straight into the kitchen to pour herself another. From the lounge came the sound of the twins laughing at a TV programme. Good. She didn't want them seeing her so upset.

What was she going to do now? She'd been lying when she said he couldn't frighten her. Actually, the thought of getting involved in a court case terrified her more than anything. Unlike Elliot, she had no money for fancy lawyers.

The phone rang again. Who was it this time? Perhaps Alan Lincoln was ringing to tell her that it was probably best all round if she forgot all about the sale. But what was she going to say to Patrick next time he rang and asked how far she'd got with putting the house on the market? And how would she tell the kids that they were going to have to sell up?

She let it ring for a long time before picking up.

'I'm sorry. I was too hasty.' It was Elliot again. 'Lowri, look, why don't you come and see me? We can discuss this business face to face.'

Go back to Wales? She hadn't been back in a long while. Most of her family had moved away years ago. There might have been the odd relative still living there, but they were so distant she could barely recall their names.

'So you can talk me out of selling the letters?'

'No. Forget about that. I've been in the States too long. It's a litigious society. Come anyway — for old times' sake.'

Next week was half term. The kids were off to the Canaries for a long weekend with their dad and the lovely Cressida — *some cheapo deal* was how Patrick had described it. If she stayed here alone she'd just be kicking her heels, worrying about the house and her ever-dwindling options. And if she didn't speak to Elliot face to face, he wouldn't know how determined she was to proceed with an auction.

'Okay,' Lowri replied. 'You're on.' *But don't think you can make me change my mind*, she added mentally after they'd said their goodbyes.

★ ★ ★

The train journey took ages. By the time Lowri arrived in Penmaerihen, having changed first at Birmingham and then at Llanlaw, it was getting dark. She was the only one to alight. She stood on the deserted platform wondering what to do next. Imagining that Elliot would probably be waiting for her outside, she headed for the exit. But there was no sign of anyone on the station forecourt either.

She heard it before she saw it — a Land Rover approaching at speed. With a squeal of brakes it came to a halt in front of her. The engine shut down and the door opened. The first thing Lowri noticed was a pair of muddy boots. Then there he was — tall, solid, dressed for the weather, apart from his head, which was bare and closely shaven.

'Oh,' she said, taken aback by the huge, scowling stranger standing in front of her.

'Miss Jenkins? I hope you haven't been waiting long.'

It wasn't a Welsh accent. Lowri took a stab at somewhere in Middle Europe — Poland, Czech Republic, some place like that. Who was he? And where was Elliot? She was about to find out.

'Elliot's been delayed, so he sent me. I was in the middle of something else so I couldn't come at once. Please accept my apologies.' He grabbed her bag and tossed it in the back of the Land Rover as if it weighed no more than a bag of sweets.

'No,' she said, 'the train was a little late. I've only just arrived.'

'Good. Good.'

If he was trying to be polite and welcoming he should have told his face, thought Lowri. He opened the passenger door and she clambered inside, strapping herself in as quickly as she could so as not to inconvenience him further.

They sped away, past the rather forlorn-looking Station Hotel with its *Rooms Vacant — Open 24 hours* sign in the window. Past the general store, where a woman in a white overall was pulling down the shutters with a long pole. Past the greengrocer's, where a dour-faced man was carrying a tray of fruit and vegetables inside.

'Quiet round these parts,' she said, for something to say.

'It is six o'clock,' he said, as if that explained it.

She shifted her gaze from the view to his hands resting on the wheel. He wore a thick gold band on his wedding finger, she noticed, and a gold stud in his ear, which looked rather metropolitan and incongruous set against the muddy boots and the rough overcoat. He drove confidently, negotiating the hairpin bends with the sort of ease that only someone used to the country roads could achieve, through the thickening dark towards the hill farm where Elliot had set up home.

They came at Llangoch Farm through a small coppiced wood. All Lowri could see at first was a dark mass. But then as they drove up the final gentle slope leading to the farm, a barrage of security lights flooded their path, illuminating a variety of buildings of different shapes and sizes.

'That's the main house,' her companion said, pointing ahead.

She guessed he meant the biggest building, taller and wider than the others, with whitewashed walls and a shingled roof.

'No car,' her companion said, pulling up in the yard. 'He isn't here yet.' He switched off the engine, jumped out and hauled her case from back of the Land Rover, directing her with a nod to follow him into the farmhouse. The first thing she noticed was the delicious aroma drifting from the kitchen. Iveta was cooking dinner, he said. If Lowri wanted to make herself comfortable in the lounge, he'd bring her a drink. Iveta was his wife, she guessed.

'This is the living room. Please, go

through and take a seat.'

And there he left her without another word. By the time half an hour had elapsed, during which time she'd finished the gin and tonic he'd brought her and scrutinised all the artefacts in the room, Lowri was about ready to call a cab and head back home. Elliot was playing mind games, she convinced herself. Sending staff to meet her, making her wait so she had plenty of time to admire her surroundings, rubbing her nose in all this opulence. Oak beams, for goodness sake! It was obviously his way of reminding her that when it came to a fight over the letters he'd win. Well, she'd see about that.

She was just thinking about how the house felt like a committee of interior designers had put it together, and how there was nothing here that told her the kind of man Elliot was anymore, when he came rushing through the door. He crossed the room and planted his hands on her shoulders, air-kissing the space on either side of her face and keeping up a stream of chatter, during which time she had plenty of opportunity to observe the change in him that the passage of time had wrought.

He looked older, naturally — just like she must do to him. But he still had his hair and in fact looked a darn sight sleeker than he'd done as a young man when he'd been prone to slouching and spots. The biggest difference was in his confident manner — the ease with which he'd greeted her, asking after her journey, wondering if she'd like another drink. He was wearing a suit that Lowri imagined probably had the name of a Savile Row tailor stitched inside. After going through the pockets and removing a fistful of business cards that he casually dropped onto the telephone table, he peeled off his elegant grey jacket and slung it over the nearest chair as if it were a skanky old sweatshirt.

The gist of his chatter, as far as Lowri could gather, was that he'd been in a planning meeting with the parish council and it hadn't gone his way. 'You'd think I was asking for permission to stage a second Glastonbury,' he said, 'not just a couple of recording studios.' He flung himself into a chair. 'The stress! God, I'm exhausted. I need a drink. And I'm hungry. You must be too.' Immediately he leapt out of the chair. 'Follow me,' he said.

The dining room was a rather chilly, overly formal room. The meal was brought in by Iveta, whom Lowri managed to get a good look at, even though the lighting in this room was so subtle it was a miracle she didn't slop the soup — which was spicy and warming and perfectly delicious — onto the crisp white tablecloth. Iveta shared a similar build with the man who was presumably her husband — and his surliness, too — ignoring Lowri completely and practically glaring at Elliot when he complained that the white wine was too cold. If he'd been here when he'd said he would, then it would have been just right, she said, with a toss of her thick, dark brown hair. As she strode out of the room her cheekbones practically sliced the air in front of her.

'Temperamental,' Elliot said, pulling a

face. He went to top up Lowri's glass but she declined. She needed to keep a clear head.

'Well I will.' He refilled his glass. 'I don't usually drink so much. It's just this business this afternoon.'

'Why don't you tell me about it?' she asked him.

It was the cue for him to complain about the locals. Maybe it had been a mistake to come back here, he said. He'd forgotten how small-minded and bigoted people in these parts were. 'Of course I'll appeal,' he said. 'There must be somebody on that planning committee who knows what a gift horse is when they see one.'

'Well, I hope it goes your way,' she said, growing tired of the subject. 'But I didn't come all this way to talk about your recording studio, Elliot.'

Elliot looked slightly taken aback. 'Do we need to talk about this now?' he said. 'Here, have some more wine. Let's have a chat about the old days. You know, I still feel terrible the way I cut you off like that.' He looked across the table at her with a mournful expression in his eyes. 'I was young and stupid.'

'That's all in the past, Elliot,' she said, brushing away their shared past with a wave of her hand. 'I'd like to talk about the future security of myself and my family. It'd be nice to get your approval to sell the letters. But if I don't get it I'll sell anyway. It's the only way I can hang on to my house.'

Elliot put a hand over hers. Good God, was he trying to seduce her? She decided she might as well leave it there till she'd heard what he had to say.

'I have a proposition,' he said after a long pause, during which Lowri struggled not to extricate her hand from beneath his. 'How much do you need, Lowri? What if I get my chequebook right now and just write down a figure? That way I can hang on to my privacy and you can keep your precious semi.'

He sat opposite her, fixing her with a cheerful smile, like he expected her to bite off his hand in gratitude. The room was silent but for a ticking clock, but then into the mix came the purring of a distant car.

Then the security lights came flooding on, dazzling both of them.

The car door slammed, then someone rang the bell. There were footsteps; the door opening; voices. A couple of minutes later Iveta came into the room.

'It's Councillor Caradoc Pryce,' she announced with a flicker of her eyes. 'I've shown him into your study.'

Don't mind me, Lowri thought. *I've already been hanging around half the evening to have this conversation with Elliot. I may as well spend the rest of it hanging around some more.*

Elliot looked suddenly pleased with himself. 'Well, well, well,' he said, 'this is a turn-up.' Turning to Lowri, he excused himself before addressing Iveta. 'Please make sure my friend has coffee served in the living room,' he said. 'And some of those delicious petit fours you make.'

And then he was gone, leaving her alone with Iveta, who, with great efficiency, began to clear the table. Lowri, determined not to let Iveta see just how annoyed she was at being abandoned for the second time this evening, rose from the table. 'I'll go and wait for my coffee then,' she said stiffly.

Iveta didn't reply, but her sly smile said it all. Back in the living room Lowri's case and coat were still where she'd left them, thankfully. Equally luckily, in among the business cards Elliot had piled up on the telephone table, she found one with the number of a taxi firm on it.

She dialled it and as she waited for someone to pick up, she found herself riffling through the other cards and reading what was on them. According to the kids, she'd read the back of a sauce bottle if it was the only available reading matter in the house.

Elliot obviously had a lot of business contacts. Were these the kind of people he hung out with these days? Builders, architects, interior designers. Oh, here was a card with the name of Caradoc Pryce on it, the visitor now locked in some kind of intense discussion with Elliot in his study, if the sound of lowered voices coming from the room was anything to go by. There was something written on the back of it that Elliot must have scribbled there.

Try him, it said in Elliot's scribble. *He might bite.*

'Speedy Taxis.'

Lowri ordered a taxi immediately to take her to the Station Hotel. She'd meet it on the road, she told the controller. She had no intention of remaining in this house a moment longer.

Dragging her case behind her, she hurried off, cursing the security lights that were bound to draw attention to her departure. Soon she was on the road, heading back in the direction she'd been driven by Martin the Morose. It had started to rain now — that fine wetting Welsh drizzle she knew so well from her girlhood. But she would not be tempted to go back.

Your precious semi, he'd said, with such contempt in his voice. Well, he was right there. It *was* precious. It was the only thing she owned in the world. And she wanted to keep it. But not if it meant going cap in hand to Elliot and accepting his charity. As soon as she got to the hotel she'd search out a computer and google

Alan Lincoln, and ask if he could recommend another auctioneer if he wasn't prepared to take her on himself.

The chugging of a car behind her made her turn round. It was the Land Rover. Lowri quickened her steps but to no avail. It had already caught her up. Iveta's other half wound down the window and spoke to her calmly, as if it was perfectly reasonable that she should have taken herself off within two hours of having arrived and without letting anyone know.

'Please. You need to get in. It's raining. I can take you where you want to go.'

'It's fine. I called a taxi,' she said.

'The taxi company rang back. The driver had a puncture. He won't be turning out again tonight.'

'There's only one taxi driver and one taxi in the whole of this area?' Lowri was dumbfounded.

'Well, look around. Sheep don't need taxis.' He had a point.

'Okay,' she said grudgingly. 'The Station Hotel.'

In the end Lowri had been forced to wait to google Alan Lincoln's name till the following evening, when she was safely back in her own home. The Station Hotel might be open twenty-four seven, but the internet connection there kept much shorter hours.

He was easy enough to find, however, with his colourful website which was a lot less reverential than that of Partridge and Page, her first port of call. Before she could change her mind she dropped him an email, leaving her contact details.

He called her the very next morning. Their conversation was brief and to the point. In her email Lowri had asked him if he could put her in touch with someone else who might be willing to auction off the letters for her, if he felt his allegiance lay with Elliot. He was very quick to dispel this notion — much to Lowri's surprise and delight. He had no allegiance to Elliot or anyone else for that matter, except his business and his clients, he was at pains to point out. All he'd done was give Elliot a ring to check the provenance of the letters. You got all sorts of people pretending to be who they weren't in his business, he said.

'When I knew you were bona fide I hoped you'd get back to me,' he added.

'You did?' she breathed. 'And you're willing to sell them?'

'Can't wait,' he said. 'How soon can we meet up and get the ball rolling?'

'Soon as you like.'

He'd need to see the letters of course, he said. But if it wasn't convenient for her to come to his office in London, then he could just as easily come to her. That might be best, she agreed. She'd had rather enough of rail journeys for the moment.

'What about the day after tomorrow then?'

★   ★   ★

When, a few hours after she herself arrived home, the children returned from their trip, Lowri quickly filled them in. They'd heard of Rubicon, of course — who hadn't? — and knew of her romance with Elliot. They knew about the

202

letters too, and that they were kept in the shoebox on top of the wardrobe with all their mother's other souvenirs.

She'd been a bit worried, however, that they might object to the publicity that an auction like this might attract. Kids were unpredictable. They were happy enough to expose their whole lives on Facebook and Twitter, but when it came to their mothers revealing that they'd once had a life that other people might be interested in — well that might be another matter.

She was going to have to broach the subject carefully, she realised. Make it less about her and more about them. It did the trick. When she told them that Alan Lincoln had said the money the letters raised might be enough not only to secure the roof over all their heads but that it might even go some way to financing the two of them through university, they were sold.

Half-term week was fast coming to an end. Today Alan Lincoln would be arriving. Lowri rose early, determined to blitz the house, which had descended into its usual squalor whenever all three of them hunkered down together for longer than a couple of days.

With the bathroom sparkling and the kitchen equally pristine, she decided she might as well nip to the supermarket before her visitor turned up. She tried to picture Alan Lincoln her head. Would he like cake? she wondered. Or was he more of a savoury man? She decided to get both types of food to be on the safe side.

As she let herself back into the house a couple of hours later, her arms full of shopping, she felt carefree for the first time in ages. Patrick had said nothing more to her about putting the house on the market when he dropped off the twins, which added to her good mood. And on top of this, after a single phone message in which he'd expressed his opinion that it had been very childish to run off like that just because he'd left her for a few minutes, there'd been nothing more from Elliot. She hoped it was a sign that he'd decided to give in gracefully.

She'd have loved to see his face when he realised that she'd done a runner — driven to the Station Hotel by his own driver, in fact! Martin. She'd found out his name in the end because she wanted to thank him and remember his kindness. It would have been a long walk in the dark and wet.

A lonely walk on a lonely road. But more time spent with you and my head will explode.

She laughed. Where did they spring from, these words? She was starting to think of the next line just as Felix came bounding down the stairs.

'Checked your messages, Mum?' he asked, reaching for her bags.

'Let me get my coat off,' she sighed. 'What's up? Hugh Jackman been pestering me for a date again?'

She wandered through to the kitchen, Felix at her heels.

'Better than that,' he said. He began to unpack the bags and put the stuff away. 'You should have bought some champagne instead of this cheap plonk.'

Lowri took out her phone. There *was* a new message in fact. From Alan Lincoln to say he should be at the house some time after two.

' . . . only it was a woman,' Felix was saying.

'What, love?' She'd been so busy fantasising about this meeting that she hadn't caught a word of anything Felix had said.

'Keep up, Mum,' Felix said. 'It wasn't the man who came for the letters. It was a woman.'

'What do you mean? Nobody's coming for them till after lunch,' she said. 'I had a message today from Alan Lincoln. Here, look.' She thrust her phone under Felix's nose.

He looked puzzled. 'She said he was tied up so she'd come instead.'

Alarm bells were beginning to ring in Lowri's head. 'Did you let a stranger into the house?' she said. 'Without checking with me first?'

'But she said . . . She showed me a business card . . . said she was his partner. Otherwise I wouldn't have . . . '

There was fear in his eyes. 'Wouldn't have what, Felix?' But already she knew the answer. It was the one she'd dreaded most.

'Otherwise I wouldn't have let her take the letters away,' he said. 'I'm so, so sorry, Mum. I can't believe how stupid I've been.'

They sat at the kitchen table, two bags of shopping still unpacked between them. Lowri knew she ought to try to comfort her son, who less than ten minutes ago had been bright-eyed with excitement. But she was still struggling to come to terms with what he'd just told her.

'She sounded genuine. She knew your name. And Elliot's. And she flashed me a card.'

These few phrases had become his mantra. It was as if he thought that if he repeated them often enough she might start to believe he'd done the right thing. That everyone would have done exactly as he'd done — invited some stranger in before nipping upstairs for the family heirloom and handing it over with a smile.

'What did you do with her card?' Lowri asked.

A pink flush of embarrassment spread over Felix's downy cheeks. 'I . . . I . . . '

207

He hadn't even read it. Let alone taken it from her. Oh, the sweet innocence of youth.

'Can you describe her, then?'

'She was foreign,' Felix sniffed. 'Tall. Big hair. Big everything, actually.'

Iveta. She should have known. Elliot must have sent her. He couldn't buy the letters so he thought he'd steal them instead. Just wait till she got him on the phone. She imagined how he'd react to her fury — calmly, politely, reminding her once more just by his confident tone that he possessed the kind of power to rustle up minions to do his dirty work. Already she could hear the smirk in his voice. No, she couldn't face it.

Felix had been doing his best to hold in his tears but now a sudden loud sob escaped. Immediately Lowri was at his side, hugging him and trying to reassure him that what had happened wasn't his fault. But her soft words were to no avail. He simply pushed her roughly away.

'Don't be like that, Felix. Honestly, I'm not cross with you. It could just as easily have been Megan who handed them over,' she said.

This, of course, was something Megan, who'd arrived in the middle of their exchange and who'd been observing its progress in incredulous silence from the doorway, strenuously denied.

'You're joking! I wouldn't have been so gullible.' Her voice dripped with contempt.

Lowri gave her a glare that immediately shut her up. Felix glared even harder. Leaping up from his chair he strode out of the room, pushing Megan — who squealed in protest — out of the way. Then he was gone, his heavy footsteps sending shudders up the staircase.

Lowri longed to rush after him. But it would be a mistake. Nothing she could say would change his view that he'd messed up badly. Somehow he would have to come to terms with it in his own way. She just hoped he wouldn't do anything stupid.

'Well, I hope you're proud,' she said, turning on Megan. 'Can't you see what a state he's in without making it worse?'

'I'm sorry,' Megan said, adding after a contrite pause, 'So, what do we do now? Get the police?'

'What could they do?' Lowri said. 'She'll have burned the letters by now on Elliot's orders.'

'Well if she has then that's a crime,' Megan countered. 'Those letters belong to you. She stole them.' She seemed momentarily cheered by the prospect of justice being served.

Unfortunately, Lowri was of another opinion. But she didn't intend to voice it. Heaven only knew what it might do to poor Felix's already shattered self-esteem if she were to say what she really believed and Megan let it slip to Felix.

Which was that the police might not see things the same way as Megan. In fact, they were probably far more likely to conclude that if anyone could be accused of taking something that didn't belong to them, her poor gullible son was just as culpable as Iveta.

★ ★ ★

This was far too urgent for Facebook. Gaz was notorious for missing important stuff because checking his messages had slipped his mind while he was in the middle of playing whatever mindless game he was currently obsessed with. Felix needed to get hold of his best friend now, while it was still light and while one more day of half term still remained.

He punched in Gaz's number, whiling away the moments before his friend picked up by chewing his nails. *Don't go to message*, he willed his phone. He was in far too much of a state to be able to leave a cogent message.

All he knew was that he'd made a Grade One idiot of himself. Because of him they were going to lose the house, and his mum would hate him for the rest of her life. It was up to him to sort it.

But he couldn't do it alone. Gaz had a car. More importantly, he was up for anything. Always had been. They'd known each other since the first day at nursery and had been pretty inseparable ever since. If there was the possibility of chasing a train all the way to Wales and confronting this Iveta when she got off it, then Gaz would be up for it. *Well* up for it!

He hated being 17. You couldn't do anything off your own bat. If he was living in an American movie he'd have his own car and a tank full of petrol outside. Not to mention a reckless spirit to match.

But he wasn't, so he had to borrow both the car and the reckless spirit from his oldest friend. He thanked his lucky stars he had a dad who felt so guilty for walking out on his family that he felt compelled to hand over fistfuls of cash at every available opportunity. At least he'd be able to supply the petrol money.

'Hey, fella. What's up?'

The first part of Felix's prayer had been answered. Now for the next.

'Dude,' he said, 'how are you fixed for a car chase?'

★ ★ ★

There was no point ringing Alan Lincoln to tell him not to bother making the journey since he was already on his way.

The least Lowri could do was show him the copies she'd made when he finally got here. Although he'd probably laugh in her face. She doubted they'd make even one fraction of the money the genuine article would in an auction.

She was still worried about Felix. Half an hour ago she'd seen Gaz's old roadster pull up outside the house. Two minutes later Felix, no doubt alerted by a text message, had come racketing down the stairs and left the house, slamming the front door behind him hard enough to make the foundations shake. They'd driven off heaven knew where, and heaven knew when he'd be back, either.

It was at times like this — dealing with a teenage boy who clammed up whenever things got difficult for him — that she wished she wasn't a single parent. Felix still *had* a father, of course. But Patrick wasn't here. Besides, he'd always preferred to be his children's best friend rather than the responsible parent, which was the role that had always fallen to her. If only Felix found it as easy to open up to her as Megan did.

Megan was with her now, drifting in and out of the living room with her iPod in her ears, pretending to be unconcerned by everything that had just happened but making sure that Lowri knew she, at least, had no plans to run away in a strop.

★   ★   ★

'I've filled the tank and input the name of the village into the sat nav. I've worked out we've got a four-hour-max drive ahead. Three if we push it.' Gaz, eyes straight ahead, tapped his thick, stubby fingers on the wheel in time to the rhythm of the house music he was playing at full volume.

'Push it then,' Felix said.

While he'd been waiting for Gaz to turn up he'd checked up on the trains. Taking into account the two changes Iveta would have to make and the long waiting time between each one, there was a chance — albeit a slim one — that they'd get to Penmaerihen first. Of course, once they got to the village they still had to find the farm. Plenty of time

214

to think about that, he decided, turning his attention back to Gaz.

'Did you grab some food?' he asked.

'In the back.'

'Ace. I couldn't get anything or Mum would have been suspicious.'

'No worries.'

The thing about Gaz was that he rarely asked questions. There was no, *What's all this about?* No, *Don't you think you should have let your mum know where you're going?* And none of the, *Have you thought about what you can really achieve here?* kind of questions he was bound to have got if he'd asked for help from any of his girl friends who could drive. Why couldn't women understand that if you wanted to discuss something, you'd discuss it? And if you kept quiet it was because you didn't feel like talking.

'I suppose you wanna know what this is all about?' he said gruffly, because suddenly he really felt the need to share.

Gaz shrugged. 'We got all afternoon,' he said.

'In that case, do you mind if I change the music? This is giving me a headache.'

∗ ∗ ∗

When a downcast Lowri first opened the door to Alan Lincoln, she hadn't known what to expect. Now all three of them sat in the living room drinking tea, the photocopies she'd had the foresight to make in a neat pile on the coffee table.

He was a grizzled bear of a man she guessed to be somewhere in his mid-sixties. Having spoken to him on the phone, she'd picked up only a trace of a Birmingham accent. But the more agitated he grew, the stronger it became.

'I should never have rung him in the first place,' he said once he'd heard Lowri's explanation of the events of the morning. 'But I like being straight with people. Sometimes I get these mad ideas that everyone feels the same way as I do about doing business. One of these days I'll learn.'

'Don't blame yourself,' Lowri said. 'It's bad enough Felix walking around with his chin on the floor. I can't cope with two people's guilt. And anyway, if anyone's to blame it's me, for not putting them in a safer place.'

'You couldn't possibly have predicted what a slimy toad Elliot had become over the years,' he said. 'No offence, if you still have feelings for him.'

'Oh I have feelings all right,' Lowri said. 'But not the sort you mean.'

Alan glanced sympathetically at her over his mug.

'I've been thinking about this studio business,' Lowri said. 'When I was there some councillor turned up. Elliot had been really down, but as soon as his visitor was announced he perked up no end. Said something about how he might have someone on his side at last. Someone with the kind of clout that could persuade others that this studio complex would be a good thing for the area.'

Alan looked interested.

'I've been wondering,' she continued. 'Is he worried that if the contents of the letters get out he might lose the support of the one person he's managed to get on his side?'

'Talk of wild parties, you mean?' Alan said.

'Exactly. Plus he says some very uncomplimentary things about his fellow Welshmen.' She reached out and grabbed one of the pages at random. '*Narrow-minded. Prudish. Stuck in the last century*,' she quoted. 'Oh, here's a good one. *Their idea of a good time round here is a trip to chapel twice a day on a Sunday.*'

Up till this moment Megan had simply sat there, picking up one page after another, reading it intently, then returning it to the pile. 'It can't just be that,' she said now, raising her eyes from the page on her lap. 'He wasn't even twenty when he wrote that stuff. Of course he was going to shoot his mouth off in a letter. It's what you do. And actually, it's nothing to what people say on Facebook and Twitter these days.'

Alan and Lowri exchanged a glance of mutual support for being so ancient.

'*And* he was an aspiring rock star,' Megan added. 'Behaving like an idiot is pretty much a prerequisite for the job, isn't it?'

Lowri stared at her daughter. When did she get to be so smart? she wondered.

'I think Megan's got a point,' Alan said. 'There's got to be something else there. Some dynamite that Elliot really doesn't want to get out.'

'But that's ridiculous. I'd have noticed, surely.'

'Only if you knew what you were looking for,' Alan said.

'There's nothing for it, then.' There was a look of grim determination on Megan's face. 'We're going to have to sit here and go through them with a fine-toothed comb until we find something.'

* * *

Martin had promised his sister he'd pick her up at the station on her return from her shopping trip to Birmingham. But the train was running late. According to her last text message it wasn't due for another half-hour, which still gave him time to check on the dogs and to make sure that the alarms were properly set since Elliot was out tonight — wining and dining another prospective ally no doubt, though much good would it do him.

He found himself dwelling on the last time he'd been to the station to pick someone up. Elliot's ex-girlfriend, so Iveta had told him jealously. She had some personal letters of Elliot's and was threatening to sell them, so Elliot had invited her down to persuade her not to.

Iveta had been in such a mood that night, banging pots and pans about and bristling with resentment about the fact that this evening she'd be waiting on some female who, she was convinced, would be taking her place in Elliot's bed later while she played the role of servant — incidentally, the only role she was paid money to carry out. The other role, as Elliot's on/off mistress, she did through slavish devotion and — Martin guessed — love.

Though what there was to love about Elliot he couldn't imagine. As far as he was concerned Elliot was the worst kind of fool — the kind that fooled himself, thinking he was smarter than everyone else. But he should have done as he,

Martin, did, and drink down at the local pub instead of up here at the farm in isolated splendour. He'd soon learn what people hereabouts really thought of him and his plans to change the nature of the farm. They'd take his money all right, and drink with him too, these councillors. But they were farmers and countrymen to the core. Elliot was wasting his time if he thought he could buy their loyalty — a loyalty that would always lie with the soil that had bred them. He understood how they felt about that. He was a son of the soil himself. A farm must stay a farm.

She must have seen through him too — the old girlfriend with the beautiful name. Lowri. A woman with spirit, walking out into the night like that. He'd made it all up, of course, about the phone call from the taxi firm about the puncture. But he'd wanted to try again because he'd failed so spectacularly to have any sort of conversation with her the first time they'd driven along this road.

He knew exactly how he must have come across — ignorant and rude. How could she know that it was her presence that had made him tongue-tied? But things were no better on the return journey. Worse in fact. Because Elliot had made her angry, and the anger came off her in waves. All she wanted, her body language told him, was to be left alone. And so he'd left her alone.

Martin looked up at the sky. He looked forward to the dark descending here in a way he never did in the city. Nightfall brought such peace. The stars here were so bright; the sky so black. But then, out of the shadows of the coppice, two figures emerged. Martin froze. No one was expected. Elliot wasn't here. There was just him and the dogs, who were already setting up a clamour.

'Hey,' he cried out, 'stop exactly where you are or I'll set the dogs on you. You're trespassing.'

He could see them more clearly now. Two young boys. One tall and skinny; frightened. The other shorter, stockier, full of bravado.

'We've come to see Elliot,' this one yelled, thrusting out his chin. 'He's got something that belongs to my mate's mother. And we want it back.'

★ ★ ★

They must have read every single letter at least three times each by now. Lowri's head was throbbing. She checked her phone again. Still no message from Felix. Obviously he was still sore at her. She thought about giving Gaz's mum a ring to see if he was round there, but thought better of it.

She had to trust him to be sensible. He was almost 18, after all. But there'd been something so . . . alien about him as he'd gone storming off upstairs. She could almost touch the testosterone radiating from him, and she had nothing to combat it with.

She slipped out to the kitchen and poured herself a glass of water. Both Alan and Megan seemed to be enjoying this. They were treating the whole business like some sort of parlour game, it seemed to her.

Words like leaves drifting from the sky,

Empty treasures of days gone by. She told herself to snap out of it. This was no time for self-indulgence. What she needed now was to think practically, not waste her time conjuring up stupid lyrics for songs that would never be written.

As soon as Alan left she'd get in touch with the estate agents. Paul had won. Elliot had won. She was going to have to put her house on the market after all. There was no magical solution to her financial problems and she'd been a fool to think there ever would be.

Alan's voice roused her from her gloomy pondering. 'Lowri! You couldn't come in here for a sec, could you? Only, there's something here I'd like to ask you about.'

'What is it?'

'Well, I don't know. But you might.'

She sighed, finished off her water and returned to the other room.

'I wanted to read you this,' Alan said, holding up a page and waving it at her. 'It's dated August 30th 1985.'

'Go on,' Megan urged. 'We're all ears.'

Alan cleared his throat. ' "Those words

you sent me. Definitely going to weave them into a couple or three songs. I was really struggling, so thanks. They were much better than anything I could ever come up with. As far as writing love songs goes, I'm still at the moon in June stage. But you make it sound real. Like it's coming from the heart. Like poetry, even. Did I say we've come up with a title? *Rubicon — The First Album*. Not very original, but hey!''

Alan looked up from the page and fixed Lowri with a questioning gaze. She hadn't a clue what she was meant to say. 'So I helped Elliot with his lyrics. I did it all the time when we were together,' was what she settled on. She didn't add that she still wrote lyrics in her head sometimes and even wrote them down when she was in the mood. A woman her age.

'You did?' Megan asked. 'You never said!'

'It would have looked like boasting,' she murmured, embarrassed. 'But they're there all right. On *The First Album*, *woven into a couple or three songs*, like he says.'

'Which ones?' Megan wanted to know.

'It was a long time ago,' Lowri hedged, 'but I think I wrote some of 'Messing With My Head'. And the chorus for 'Down Time'. And most of 'Don't Say Those Things'.'

'Do you know what I think?' Alan looked at them both intensely. 'I think the real reason he doesn't want those letters in public view is this. When it gets out that he hasn't come up with those lyrics on his own, someone — say a lawyer, or say me for instance — will tip you off that if you wrote those words, as this letter suggests, then you might be entitled to royalties.'

'Really?' Lowri was suddenly struck dumb.

'That's right,' Alan said. 'All we have to do now is come up with the proof.'

Alan was such an optimist he made everything sound so easy. What did it matter anymore if the letters were no longer in her possession? he said. There was no need for an auction now anyway. The copies she'd taken would be plenty good enough to pursue her claim through the law. All she needed was to prove that the words in those three songs had been penned by her, contradicting Elliot's claims that he was the sole lyricist. But how on earth was she supposed to dig up such evidence after all these years? Suddenly things didn't seem quite so cut and dried.

'These were words scribbled on the back of an envelope,' she said. 'Spoken over the phone. It's my word against his.' Suddenly they were back to square one. 'Look, Alan,' Lowri added, 'I appreciate your support in all this, I really do. But I think we just have to accept that the game's up. Elliot's just too big for us to take on.'

Determined not to show just how deflated she felt, Lowri set to with a vengeance, sweeping up the empty mugs and plates and carrying them off into the kitchen, where she applied herself to the task of the washing up as if her life depended on it.

'Mum.'

She was making such a clatter that she hadn't heard Megan arrive. 'Yes, darling?'

she said in a voice artificially bright.

'You know that big box of old videos you kept meaning to throw out when video recorders became extinct? *Did* you throw it away?'

Megan's question took Lowri by surprise. 'It's probably still up in the little front room with all the other rubbish,' she said. 'But why do you want to know?'

'Might be a long shot,' Megan said. 'But I distinctly remember one with you singing with two other girls. I used to play it all the time when I was a kid. One girl played the guitar and you and the other girl sang.'

'That's right! Somebody filmed us for the final of the college talent contest!' she exclaimed. 'Me, Josie and Sandy. Sandy played the guitar, Josie sang, and I sort of did the chorus. Fancy you remembering that!'

Megan eyed her mother warily. 'Do you remember what you performed?'

Lowri felt bubbles of excitement start to rise. 'Not exactly. But I do know we performed our own material. In fact, that's why we won. Elliot and his band

— I think they called themselves Butt Out back then — just did cover versions, you see, and came second because of it.'

She'd written the words herself, and between all three of them they'd come up with the tune. Elliot had been furious when they'd come second because he'd been so sure that he and his group were going to win. She'd told him he was a jerk and thought that was the end of that, but next day during break he'd been waiting for her outside her classroom. That had been the start of their relationship.

A couple of years later she'd returned to those songs when Elliot had told her he was struggling to come up with a lyric to match the music he'd written. Maybe she'd changed the odd line, but no more than that.

'Run upstairs and have a hunt through the box to see if you can find it,' Lowri said. 'You never know!'

Megan was already out of the room. Lowri, unable to bear the wait, threw down her tea towel. 'Wait for me,' she yelled. 'I'm coming too!'

The big man with the closely shaven head and the single earring had marched both of them into the living room. He stood in front of the huge fireplace, his thick arms folded across his broad chest and his feet planted sturdily apart. He looked like someone you'd be well advised not to upset. Though from the barely imperceptible pulsing of the blue vein just above his left eyebrow, it might already be too late.

' . . . so we came the rest of the way on foot,' Gaz was saying.

Felix wished he'd shut up. He was sure that when their captor had asked where'd come from and how they'd got here, all he'd wanted was a quick answer, not a blow-by-blow account of their route. Now Gaz was detailing their problems with the car, which had finally died on them about a quarter of a mile away.

'So you say that someone — a woman who said she knew Elliot and that she'd been sent by Alan Lincoln, a man she said was her partner — came into your house and took away some letters that belonged to your mother?' He glared at Felix as if it were his fault he'd been robbed.

'Yes,' he mumbled.

'And you think this woman lives here?'

'My mum *knows* she does,' Felix said. Thinking of his mum and how nice she'd been to him when he really didn't deserve it encouraged him to stand his ground. 'She says she's called Iveta.'

The blue vein pulsed more strongly. Felix could hear his heart knocking against the wall of his chest and wondered if any second now it might just stop altogether. All things considered that might be for the best.

He had been half-aware of another sound in parallel to his laboured heartbeat — that of a car approaching. Now it finally pulled up somewhere outside. There was the sound of doors slamming and a man and a woman speaking in low voices. Then footsteps, a key in the door. Finally, laughter spilling into the hall.

The big man followed the direction of the sound with narrowed eyes. His arms hung by his side but he was clenching his fists. It suddenly occurred to Felix that his fury wasn't so much directed at Gaz and him but at whoever it was on the other side of that door.

Which turned out to be the woman who'd knocked on his own door this morning. Elliot couldn't believe it! They'd actually achieved what they'd set out to achieve. Except — what the heck were they supposed to do now?

She was with a man that Felix knew could only be Elliot Hogan. When all this about the letters and the auction had come up he'd googled him. And though he was older than the pictures online, you could still see the young man in him if you looked hard enough.

He looked rather irritated, Felix thought. As if he'd come home expecting an evening in front of the box with a six-pack and a pizza and now here were all these people cluttering up his space.

'Who on earth are these people?' Elliot addressed the big man, who looked like thunder.

'Why don't you ask Iveta?' Martin replied, his voice cold.

Elliot glanced at Iveta questioningly. But Iveta simply shrugged and gave an odd smile, as if the intruders were of little account. Felix felt like punching her.

'I was expecting a call to come and pick you up,' Martin said.

'Oh, it wasn't necessary in the end,' she replied. 'Elliot called me on the train and offered since he wasn't far away.'

'So how was your shopping trip? Need a hand with your bags, or have you left them in the car?'

Iveta sighed. 'Oh for goodness sake, Martin. I'm tired of these games. You *know* I didn't go on any shopping trip because this boy here — ' She jabbed her manicured finger in Felix's direction. ' — has told you where I really went.'

At her words Elliot did a double take. Felix felt his face go hot.

'What? This is him? The kid who gave you the letters? Lowri's boy?'

Iveta began to laugh. It was a high-pitched peal at odds with her speaking voice, which was deep and smoky. She opened her bag with a flourish, pulling out the bundle of letters.

'I'm guessing you've come for these,' she said.

Felix stood there rooted to the spot as she began to wave them in his face tauntingly. It was as if she dared him to come closer and take them from her.

He made a grab for them but she stepped back, laughing even louder. Felix was furious now. He was dimly aware of the big man angrily saying something in a language he didn't understand and Iveta equally angrily saying something back.

But their fury was nothing compared to Felix's. Unable to restrain himself any longer, he lurched towards her. But then he caught his foot on the leg of the stupid telephone table that was in his way and tripped, falling forward. He was dimly aware of an oak beam coming towards him. He heard a crack as he felt the blow. Then he slid to the floor, landing in a heap at Iveta's feet. The last thing he remembered was Iveta's face looking down at him, her eyes wide and her mouth a round O with shock.

★ ★ ★

They'd rummaged in that dusty old box for a long time. The glee that had overtaken them when they'd found what they were looking for had completely wiped out all memory of the despair Lowri had felt earlier in the day, when she'd arrived home to find the letters had gone.

Even though she hadn't seen what was on it, she felt certain it was the one they were looking for. And despite Alan's warning that if the magnetic coating on the tape had been removed through constant replay it might not be possible to digitize the recording, and in that case they'd be back were they started, her good mood didn't change. *Just do your best, Alan, please*, she'd said as she wished him goodbye.

She'd gone to bed, imagining him watching the tape on his old video machine — she ought to have known just from looking at him that he was a hoarder — and waiting for his call. Unable to sleep, she'd finally given up trying.

Now she sat by the fire, mug in hand, waiting for something to happen. The lateness of the hour and the silence in the house combined forces with each other to nibble away at her optimism, revealing it to be a frail cover. Now new concerns took over — worries about the whereabouts of Felix that hitherto she'd managed to keep harnessed. He still hadn't called. She'd rung his mobile half a dozen times but it had gone straight to answer phone. When she'd finally succumbed to ringing Gaz's mum she'd got nowhere. Gaz was out but he hadn't said where he was going or when he'd be back, was all his mum had said. But then almost as if she'd summoned up a call by her very thoughts, her mobile rang.

It was Alan. 'I've just sent you an email,' he said. 'Click on the URL. Tell me if you recognise these lyrics. Because I sure do.'

It was with a beating heart that Lowri obeyed his instructions. She held her breath as the video loaded and began to play. Suddenly there they were, the three of them. Her oldest friends, both of whom she'd lost touch with. Josie had emigrated to New Zealand in her early twenties. Initially they'd corresponded, but over the years their correspondence had dwindled to nothing. As for Sandy, she had no idea what had happened to her.

But for ten whole minutes the three of them were back together, singing and playing their hearts out. 'Don't Say Those Things' was the first song they sang. The tune was derivative and frankly cringeworthy. But the words weren't bad. Elliot must have agreed, otherwise he wouldn't have accepted them so easily.

Don't tell me you love me; don't tell me you care.

Words that vanish like a puff of air.

Just back me up and don't put me down,

Don't question my choices, never mess me around.

Lowri pressed pause. She needed to retrieve her copy of *The First Album* from her vinyl collection. In a moment she was back, checking the words on the back of the album cover against the words Josie sang. She did the same with 'Messing With My Head' and 'Down

237

Time', the two songs that followed.

Those were her words all right. Of course, she'd known it twenty years ago when Rubicon's first album had first been released. But it had never occurred to her that she might be entitled to payment when she'd given Elliot those lyrics. They'd been a gift from her to the boy she loved.

She didn't love him any longer though. She loved her kids and the idea of keeping a roof over their heads. How could he, knowing how desperate she was for funds, be so mean as to deceive her about what she was owed?

Immediately she typed a reply to Alan. *Do you know a good lawyer?* she wrote. *Because I'm up for a fight*. Seconds later his reply appeared. *You're in luck*, it said. *Dave Lincoln deals with all my legal affairs*. She typed back, *Familiar name*. And back came the reply, *He's my brother*.

She was just laughing at the smiley face that accompanied his words when her landline rang. Her stomach did a somersault. It was bound to be bad news

238

about Felix. Jettisoning her laptop, she ran to the phone, snatched up the receiver and identified herself.

'Lowri, I'm sorry to ring you at such a late hour. It's Martin. I work for Elliot. We met, remember?'

She waited for more.

'You mustn't worry. But Felix has had an accident. I'm ringing from the A&E department at the hospital.'

'I'm on my way.'

★　★　★

Felix, sitting in the side room he'd been allocated while waiting to be discharged, felt rather proud of his war wound. Touching the dressing on his forehead, he prayed he'd end up with a scar. He needed all the help he could get to establish some badly needed street cred at school.

Gaz had slipped out for some drinks, and Martin was on the phone to Felix's mum. Felix was totally resigned to the fact that she would, in all probability, kill him. He'd said as much to Martin, but

Martin only laughed.

It was Martin who'd brought him here after he'd knocked himself out on that oak beam. Not that he'd been out for long; and in fact he'd silently agreed with Elliot and Iveta that there was no need for a doctor. But Martin said they couldn't risk it — not with a head wound.

There was a lot more shouting too, what with Elliot complaining loudly about the blood on his soft furnishings. He'd finally stomped out the room, declaring that if Martin insisted the boy saw a doctor then he'd have to find one himself, as he had no intention of calling his own medical man out at this time of night and risking some hack getting hold of the wrong end of the stick.

Once he'd left, more words were exchanged, this time between Martin and Iveta, in that foreign language again, although it was Martin who did most of the talking. Whatever he'd said obviously affected her, because when he'd finished she ended up offering to clean Felix up. She looked sort of humble as she did it;

her touch was gentle and she kept apologising in case she was hurting him, which she absolutely wasn't. But the most amazing thing was that just as they — Gaz, Martin and himself — were getting into the car to go to the hospital, she'd come running out of the house and thrust the letters in his hands.

'I did it for Elliot,' she mumbled, unable to meet his eye. 'But they don't belong to him. Any young man who would go to such lengths to look out for his mother is ten times the man that Elliot will ever be.'

Hearing her say that made him feel less of an idiot for running into a beam. Especially when Martin nodded in agreement. He liked Martin. A damn sight more than he liked Elliot.

'Your mum wanted to come right away,' Martin said as he came back into the room where Felix was waiting. 'But there are no trains till tomorrow. I said I'd drive you both home after a good night's sleep. You can stay at my place.'

'What about my car?' Gaz, bearing two cans of coke, appeared behind him.

'Was she mad at me?' Felix asked simultaneously.

Martin made a so-so gesture with his hand. 'At first yes. But then I told her she should be proud of what you'd done and she had to agree it wasn't all bad.'

At this Felix relaxed, while Martin explained to Gaz that he'd taken a look at the car and it needed a lot of work doing to it. He'd get someone to fix it in the village, he said, and drive it back when it was ready.

'And don't worry about the money,' he added. 'Elliot will pay. I'll make sure of that.'

★ ★ ★

In the end there was no need for lawyers. Elliot had owned up. It was stupid of him, he'd said. And he hoped Lowri would forgive him. Never before had she met a man who was always so ready to apologise for his wrongdoings. It was like a disease with him.

He'd come through with an offer that far exceeded anything a one-off payment from the auctioning off of a few love letters might deliver. It had needed finessing, but Alan had been confident that there'd be little opposition from Elliot's lawyers, and he'd been right. Lowri wasn't the only person to whom Alan had sent that URL link. How she would have loved to see Elliot's face when he clicked on it and realised exactly what it was.

The house would be safe now, and soon Lowri would be in a position to buy Patrick out. Pity that he and Cressida had decided that perhaps theirs wasn't a match made in heaven after all.

Felix's forehead had been bestowed with a scar that by his own account had put up his stock immeasurably with the cool kids in his year. According to Megan, he might even have got a girlfriend out of it, if the looks that Amy-Jane Harris kept giving him whenever their paths crossed were anything to go by.

But Felix was still Felix. He could never be up for long. It was a Saturday morning and Lowri's contract had finally arrived. It was several pages long and took some reading.

'What does *in perpetuity* mean?' Felix wanted to know.

'It means that when Mum snuffs it we'll still get the royalties,' Megan, who'd recently decided that she wanted to be a lawyer, spoke through a mouthful of toast.

'Blimey!' Felix exclaimed. 'So actually, me going all that way and getting a bang on the head just for those letters was a bit of a waste of time.'

But Lowri disagreed. If it hadn't been for the letters, she'd never have been reminded that once upon a time she had a talent for writing song lyrics, she told them both. A talent that she hoped might serve her well in the future. Alan thought so at least. *There's probably not mega-bucks in it*, he'd explained. *But there's definitely bucks to be made if you can keep coming up with the goods.*

Lowri was keeping her fingers crossed about that. She was keeping her fingers crossed about something else too — that she might get another phone call from Martin, who'd continued to ask after

Felix since he'd delivered him home that day. Just to make sure there were no ill effects from his fall, he insisted.

He rang just as she was wiping away a jammy fingerprint from her brand-new contract and hoping that it wouldn't make it null and void. 'I've got some news,' he said.

It hadn't escaped her notice that he'd totally forgotten to ask about Felix. 'Good, I hope,' she replied.

'Elliot's packing up. He's selling the farm and going back to LA.'

'Really? Why's that?' Lowri wanted to know. 'Already bored with sheep farming?'

Martin explained that Elliot's plans to set up a studio had been turned down. Though he had the right of appeal, he'd already accepted that he hadn't a leg to stand on. 'He's leaving immediately. Wants me to stay on till he finds a buyer. I'm hoping the next guy who comes along is serious about farming and will keep me on as his estate manager.'

'He'd be a fool not to,' Lowri said. 'What about Iveta? Is she staying on? Or will she be following Elliot?'

Martin gave a low chuckle. 'Not likely. She's totally over him, thank God. She's off to London to stay with friends while she looks for something else. This place is far too quiet for her.'

'I think I'd like to come and see it again,' she said. 'Now that Elliot's left. It's a beautiful part of the world.'

'Come any time you like,' Martin said. 'I'd love to show you around.'

Lowri thought about it. She'd been here before, and not too long ago either. But she had a feeling that this time things would be very different.

We do hope that you have enjoyed reading this large print book.

Did you know that all of our titles are available for purchase?

We publish a wide range of high quality large print books including:
Romances, Mysteries, Classics
General Fiction
Non Fiction and Westerns

Special interest titles available in large print are:
The Little Oxford Dictionary
Music Book, Song Book
Hymn Book, Service Book

Also available from us courtesy of Oxford University Press:
Young Readers' Dictionary
(large print edition)
Young Readers' Thesaurus
(large print edition)

For further information or a free brochure, please contact us at:
Ulverscroft Large Print Books Ltd.,
The Green, Bradgate Road, Anstey,
Leicester, LE7 7FU, England.
Tel: (00 44) **0116 236 4325**
Fax: (00 44) **0116 234 0205**

Other titles in the
Linford Mystery Library:

THE COMIC BOOK KILLER

Richard A. Lupoff

Hobart Lindsey is a quiet man, a bachelor living with his widowed mother in the suburbs and working as an insurance claims agent. Marvia Plum is a tough, savvy, street-smart cop. Then fate throws the unlikely pair together. A burglary at a vintage comic book store leads to a huge insurance claim that Lindsey must investigate for his company — and to the brutal murder of the store owner, for which Marvia must find the killer. Lindsey and Plum, like oil and water — but working together to unravel a baffling mystery!

words *photo by Adele Feaver*.

'They report her missing when they get a call later on Monday morning from the sixth form college where she works. Adele Feaver hasn't turned up and has failed to call in sick. It's a mystery, especially as Monday's apparently the first day of the art department's summer exhibition and Mrs Feaver's the curator.'

Alan Togher raised his hand, catching the Super's attention immediately. Kim liked the boy very much — she'd puppy-walked him when he'd first joined the force, and to this day he still followed her around eagerly; her own personal lap dog was how Janice described him. What's a curator? he wanted to know. Patiently the Super explained it meant someone in charge of — in this case — an art exhibition.

'Don't ever be afraid to ask questions, Alan,' she added, picking up on the expressions of disdain on the faces of some of the more experienced officers. 'It's only by asking questions that we get the answers.'

Alan looked chuffed. He'd go far, that

one, Kim was convinced.

'Anyway, according to the daughter, she'd never have missed it for the world. It was her favourite time of the year.'

'So what now, ma'am?' Janice asked.

'What now is this. Three days have passed, and there's still no sign of Adele Feaver, and she's not picking up her mobile. So we're duty-bound to report her to the missing persons bureau, enter her details on the PNC for circulation nationwide, and check out any CCTV. That's just for starters.'

'House to house?' Janice enquired.

The Super nodded. 'A check of local hospital admissions, checks on her computer, and with her bank too, of course.'

'Work colleagues? They'll need talking to too, won't they?' John Farmer asked.

The Super agreed. 'Sooner or later, of course,' she added, 'if we don't find her we're going to have to apply for her dental and medical records as well as search the house.' She glanced at Kim. 'That might be a sensitive area, Kim. You need to let them know why we're doing it — that they're not under suspicion, but